# BITE OF HUNGER

# BITE OF HUNGER

## HUNGER

### A NOVEL OF AFRICA
### BY HILDA KUPER

HARCOURT, BRACE & WORLD, INC.
NEW YORK

*For my sisters*

The setting is Swaziland. Place and time are fused in my memory of this small country in southern Africa.

The story that follows is fiction, but fiction re-creates the illusions of life. The characters are known to me alone; their reality is in my perception of many people who made my world in Swaziland.

Hilda Kuper

*Los Angeles*
February, 1965

# CONTENTS

# BITE OF HUNGER

# 1 · TOO PROUD

The village was asleep in the bright sunlight. Life had spilt from the glazed bowl-shaped Swazi huts to the distant fields and pasture-lands. Only a red dust road over the pastel-shaded hills, traversed twice a week by a railway bus, linked the scattered homesteads with an unseen outer world.

A man dozed on the ground, his back against the reed fence of the yard, and near him lay a scrawny mongrel dog.

Despite the heat, both man and dog faced the fire that burnt under enormous iron cooking pots. Saliva trickled down the corners of the sleeper's half-open mouth, and the dog licked its jaws compulsively. The voices of children at the river-bank came clearly through the stillness, above the persistent reverberation of flies and the sucking of flames in logs slightly green.

At a slight extra sound, the dog leapt up, snarling, but before the man stirred, it had been silenced with a whispered command: "Shut up, Peta."

The intruder was a young girl with smooth gold-brown skin and graceful carriage. The dog flattened onto the ground and watched. She stood looking at the man, his body slack-muscled in sleep.

"Mpisi," she called, then imperiously, "Mpisi, wake."

He half-opened rheumy eyes, saw her, yawned with voluptuous extension of mouth and arms, and said thickly, "What do you want, *Nkosatana?*"

"I ache for meat."

He sat up and grinned. "We all ache for meat. Wait for tomorrow."

"I want it now." Her voice was firm. He did not notice her bare toes digging into the ground and her fingers knuckled taut.

Casually he responded, "I, too, am hungry."

He rose to push the logs farther under the pots and stirred the simmering contents.

Wet beads glowed on her forehead. She repeated, "I ache for meat. Now."

He brushed her off.

"It is not mine to give."

"I know." She retorted angrily, "It is not yours. It is my father's."

"Go ask him, then," shrugged the henchman.

She did not deign to reply, but stalked off; such shame as she knew filled her, and her firm young breasts, under a loose, gay print, sharpened at the insult.

Mpisi called, "Come back, *Nkosatana*. Come back, Lamtana."

But she took no notice, and as he watched her go through the doorway he said aloud to himself, "That girl is too proud." Then he relaxed again on the ground.

Once outside the fence, Lamtana walked slowly towards the voices of the children. She clamped her eyes to force back tears of rage. That Mpisi had been right deepened the insult. She was the daughter of a prince, Mhau Nkosi Dlamini, and Mpisi was her father's servant. She had begged from him, and he, a nobody, had rebuffed her. She hated him. She hated herself. She hated everyone.

She was about to turn back and sit by herself in her mother's hut when one of the children spied her and shouted, *"Hau,* Lamtana. What are you doing? Come and see what we've got. Hurry. It's a lovely thing."

It was no use hiding now; besides, her curiosity was aroused. The children were excitedly pressing round a tall, sweet-faced girl slightly older than Lamtana. Lamtana pushed the others aside and saw, cupped in the tall girl's hands, an ecstasy of quivering color—a small weaver-bird, its wings of vivid green sparkling through shades of blue to yellow, its head adorned with two black beauty-spots, its beak of flame.

Lamtana put out her hand and gasped. "Sicenga, give it to me."

"Wait," Sicenga replied. "We're deciding what we should do with it—kill it or let it go."

A younger girl, with mischief in her eyes, shouted gleefully, "Kill it."

Someone laughed, "Totwa, you're like a boy!"

She mocked him. "Must only boys have fun?" The others chuckled at her nonsense.

A plain-faced companion pleaded, "Please, Princess, kill it."

It was easy to pick out the royal children. Though they had different mothers, the bone of their bodies was visibly structured by their noble father. From him, too, Sicenga and Totwa had inherited the broad nose and wide-apart eyes. Lamtana, whose features were, like her mother's, finely cut, had his mouth, thick without coarseness, sensual and yet controlled.

But it was not simply the physical appearance that set the young aristocrats apart, it was their poise, a subtle shadow inculcated into them by special medicines and rituals of chieftainship. It shone through the girls' simple clothing of unsewn cloth and gave authority to their voices and gestures. It entitled them to deference from the other children, to whom, in return, they were expected to show courtesy, generosity, and consideration.

Lamtana, however, was not much concerned with her obligations; she acted directly on the knowledge that her mother, known as Nabo Lamtana, was the noblest born of all the wives in Prince Mhau's harem. And though Lamtana may have been less loved than either her older half-sister, the gentle Sicenga, or the younger, vivacious Totwa, she was now ready to assume leadership.

When asked to decide the fate of the bird, she acted entirely according to her own desires.

"Give it to me," she repeated and put her hands over Sicenga's. Resigned, Sicenga relinquished the prize.

Lamtana felt the anguished flutter within her palms, and the tickle of the clawed feet sticky from the gluelike berries used for the snare. She held the legs gently, and widened out her palms so that she could better see the beauty.

"Where did you find it?" she asked.

All the children began to answer at the same time.

"What a noise! Sicenga, tell me."

With many interruptions, Sicenga recounted how two boys, Timba and Feka, had come by on their way to the prince to tell him that a letter had come from Feka's father, Mputuya, to say he was returning from Goli (Johannesburg, the city of gold). Timba had shown the bird to the girls. When Totwa asked if they could keep it, he had given it to her, saying, and here Totwa took over, imitating Timba, "We boys aren't interested in eating butterflies."

"It's all very well for boys," Totwa continued, laughing now and coquettish, "they can hunt anything. But we girls are different. We are only allowed to cook." So she had suggested, after the boys had gone, that they roast the bird.

"It is too small to eat," said Sicenga practically.

But Lamtana was not listening. Her hands moved gently over the warm breast feathers through which the small heart throbbed. Circular seedlike eyes stared at her without expression.

"Perhaps we should kill it," Lamtana mused aloud. "I've never seen the inside of such a tiny bird."

"I've got a knife," said Totwa.

Lamtana tried to imagine the bone and blood and bits beneath the radiance. It was too perfect.

"Do it, Totwa," she decided, "kill it."

With mock solemnity, Totwa announced, "The man-of-the-council has decided. I'll be a warrior. Give it here."

Slowly, Lamtana gave it up. But she did not watch the kill, and when she looked again her face saddened. The little bird was lying still on the dry grass, and across the water-blue breast ran a thread of scarlet.

Quickly she said, "It's like any chicken," and walked away.

The children busied themselves gathering twigs for the fire. When it was ready, they would thrust their catch into the crackling flame. They did not pluck it first; if it had any substance and roasted properly, the charred feathers would break off, leaving a tasty morsel behind.

Lamtana did not attempt to help. She sat staring moodily in the direction of the village, from which rose thin spumes of smoke. As she recalled Mpisi's insolence and her own humiliation, she felt unpleasant and unaccustomed remorse. She wished she had not said "Kill it." Her shame turned into renewed anger against Mpisi. He was the meanest man in the world and the most heartless. Hadn't he let his own brother's wife, Timba's mother, nearly die of sickness and hunger?

Her mind wandered to Timba and Feka, his cousin, the two boys who had brought the bird. She knew that they would laugh when Totwa described—as she was sure to—the deliberations and the final decision. She jabbed her finger at an ant. Her thoughts skipped to Mputuya, Feka's father, and to men in general. They were lucky. If they wanted, they were able to work far away and see the world. She did not believe all the stories they told on their return to the country, but there was no doubt that in the cities people, especially whites, performed miracles. Look at the buses and motor cars, and the flymachines that she had seen on two memorable occasions, circling the sky like silver birds. Even Simon's shop, nearer home, was full of things her people couldn't make—torches like her father's, used when he went round the village at night looking for witches, and coloured bangles of glass like the ones her mother had bought her a few days back.

She suddenly felt impatient to go home.

"Haven't you finished yet?" she called out.

Sicenga replied more irritably than was her wont, "Of course. You've been dreaming. We're all ready."

"Have you eaten without calling me?"

"It was just ashes."

"Let's go," said Lamtana.

Slowly, in single file, the children walked along the path through the yellow grass. When they were near the village the wind blew towards them the delicious odour of meat.

Totwa stopped for a moment, breathing deeply.

"Ah, tomorrow. I can hardly wait."

The others began chattering happily, detailing the pleasures of feasts past and to come. It had been weeks since they had tasted beef, their favourite food, and then it had been from a lean old ox that had to be killed after it had fallen into a hole and broken a leg. Its flesh was lined with sinews, whereas the cow for the coming feast had been specially fetched from the rich grazing fields in the bush country and was big and sleek with fat.

Sicenga ruminated, "Mpisi's such a good cook; he can even make tough meat taste sweet enough."

"Anyone can cook meat," commented Lamtana coldly. "Even Mpisi. The dog."

The children gaped at her in astonishment. Sicenga quoted the proverb "A chief is a chief by his people."

Totwa mocked, "If you're so proud, and walk over others with your nose in the sky, you might fall into a hole just like an old cow and nobody will bother to dig you out."

"I will say what I like and walk where I like. And if I fall into a hole, that will be my affair." With an exasperating indifference to the opinion of others, Lamtana walked rapidly into the village.

She went straight to her mother's empty sleeping hut, crawled in, and shut the low door. Automatically she squeezed her eyes for a moment to accustom them to the darkness. Her mother's blankets hung from the rafters between two upright supporting poles, and grass sleeping mats were neatly stacked in rolls at one side. From behind the blankets, hidden in the thatching, she fetched a small key on a long string. The only solid furniture was a large tin trunk pushed against the wall farthest from the door.

Squatting in front of the trunk, she unlocked it and lifted the lid. At the top were a few folded pieces of printed cloth and under them a small tin box, which she took out very carefully. In it were six plumes of the flamingo, decorations reserved for aristocrats, and six bangles of multi-coloured glass that glittered in the dim light. Lovingly she took out the bangles and slipped three over each shapely, narrow wrist.

While she was admiring them, she heard her mother's loud voice approaching. Quickly she took off her jewels, whispering, "We will see each other tomorrow," and put all the things back in their places. When Nabo Lamtana came to her hut, Lamtana was already outside.

The resemblance between them was obvious—the same oval face, light-golden and smooth in texture, the liquid almond eyes, the clearly defined nose, the long supple neck. Only the mouth was different; Nabo Lamtana's was sulky, discontented, hard, but Lamtana's ripe raspberry lips were shaped upwards at the corners even in repose.

"What are you doing here, my child?" asked her mother, widening her eyes suspiciously and thrusting forward her small, elegant head adorned with its high pot-shaped coiffure.

"Nothing, Mother." Lamtana's tight black ringlets, like fine coiled springs, fell over her politely downcast face.

"Why do nothing behind closed doors?"

"I wanted to look again at the bangles you gave me," Lamtana burst out truthfully.

*"Hau,"* she exclaimed. "Did you put them back?"

"Of course. I will wear them tomorrow?"

"We will see." The woman's voice dropped to a whisper. "You must try not to awaken jealousy, my child. We have too many enemies. Witchcraft feeds on jealousy."

"I know, Mother."

They stood together, listening. With the setting sun, life was returning to the homestead. The shrill voices of women in public gossip leapt over the reed fences that surrounded their separate huts. Children played and ran messages. Babies cried. Grinding stones beat. The lowing of cattle surged from the open palisaded byre that stood in the centre of the homestead. An occasional encouraging whistle from the milkers pierced all other sounds. From the barracks of the young men came the latest melancholy song: "My name is left behind me with the loose girls of the city. With all of them I left my name." The smoke from the hearths seeped through the thatching.

Nabo Lamtana shrugged her shoulders. "We must cook. Fetch the corn. Tomorrow there will be meat."

"Yes. Tomorrow is near." Lamtana smiled suddenly. With the shine of the bangles in her eyes she went to fetch the corn for the meal of today.

## 2 · THE BITE OF HUNGER

The meat was Mhau's reward to his people for help in weeding his fields. He knew that the loyalty of subjects required adequate nourishment to survive. His was a poor district, growing steadily poorer as its population increased and the scrawny cattle destroyed the pasture. Sometimes only a score of men responded to his call for labour, and he had no authority to inflict punishment on defaulters or to summon to his service the many absentees who spent their prime years toiling in mines or on farms. With the passing of time he became increasingly conscious of his rivals in power—white men who paid their workers in money. The old and crippled, the women and the children —these remained. The able-bodied men who returned stayed but a short while to rest, for they had wants and values that he could neither satisfy nor understand. Only when there was a feast at his village they came in large numbers, even the young men in slick city suits, and they ate and drank their fill, temporarily united in intimate sacrament and praise songs of the chief.

All of them from the smartest to the shabbiest had suffered periodic pangs of hunger. Each year before the new crop ripened they faced the month named Swallow the Pickings of the Teeth. The greatest luxury was a feast of meat. Not just a taste, but a bellyful. To gorge on substantial flesh, to swallow the fatty gravy, to crack the bones and scrape out the marrow, to eat until they could eat no more. What a rare, exquisite sensation.

They collected in small groups in the large open space between the main huts and the cattle byre. Men sat apart from women, and cutting through the sex-based groups was age, the spear of time itself. The old men, huddled together under the council tree, cast tired, wise eyes at the youths with their large, bold bodies and their bare legs wide apart as they straddled the hard ground. Between them sat the group of married men with strength still left to spill itself in children and in work.

The wives of the chief, in traditional blackened ox-hide skirts and goatskin aprons, sat apart from the other women, many of whom wore ungainly dresses of shop cloth. Facing the chief was his first wife, Nabo Sicenga, dignified and placid, and beside her Nabo Lamtana, craning her long neck to see what guests were there, and then the softly rounded Nabo Totwa, cuddling in her arms her youngest child, a little golden son clothed in a single string of bright red beads. The children sat upright, dignified, with their own peers. The chief's children formed a separate, distinguished circle. On Lamtana's wrists gleamed the glass bangles. They shone more brilliantly than the intricately plaited armlets and anklets of yellow grass worn by her half-sisters, and she was conscious of the admiration, tempered by envy, cast in her direction.

Prince Mhau, as lord and host, stood proudly supervising the distribution of the huge joints. Advising him was Beta, his an-

cient grand-uncle and senior member of the family council, a
thin-nosed old man whose black eyes made bright slits in his
wrinkled skin. Mhau was grateful to him: he felt safer with old
men than with young; they had tradition and precedent to offer,
while the young confused him with new greeds. He was glad
that the ox-head, with its soft tongue and sweet, coiled brains,
went to the aged, who had the privilege of eating in the sacred
cattle byre itself; the tough forelegs were sent to the arrogant,
unfettered youths.

Mhau himself was in the full vigour of manhood, but he had
assumed his position as chief when still unfledged and had never
travelled beyond the protection of the small country of the
Ngwenyama (the Lion), king of the Swazi. Nor did he have any
desire to do so. He was not prepared to lose the identity of his
status. He did not want to be anonymous. In his own setting he
was—and looked—the ideal chief. He was very tall and of
enormous girth, and his head, nobly proportioned, was garlanded
with a crown of polished black wax. A khaki shirt, open at the
neck and fitting tight across the waist, hung over the spotted red-
and-white print kilt that girded his loins, reaching to his knees;
over the print flapped a triangular *lijobo* of soft buckskin. His
massive, almost hairless legs were bare except for a narrow ank-
let of medicines, and he wore no shoes on his fine strong feet.

Nabo Totwa, slightly intoxicated by beer specially brewed for
the chief, commented audibly with a sigh of longing: "I have
never seen a man like our husband." And she hugged her naked
baby to her breast in a rush of uncontrolled affection. The child
began to suckle contentedly, but Nabo Lamtana turned towards
her and, though her words were joking, her eyes were hard.

"You spoil him. Go, man, leave the milk and take the
meat."

Nabo Totwa smiled as she said, "Let him be. There's still less
meat than milk." She crooned to the baby, "Eat, my child, and
be full."

Mhau looked at his wives, and his countenance reflected the

stimulus of recollected variety. Nabo Sicenga, his first fully
known woman, was always pleasant and generous, sweet-
spoken and peace-loving, a noble influence on the younger
wives. He felt less respect and less affection for the swanlike
Nabo Lamtana. To himself he said, "She has a dangerous jealousy. She must not see to whom my heart pushes me," and then
he smiled as he watched Nabo Totwa with her baby. Perhaps
conscious of his interest, she rose and looked at him long and
tenderly, then tied her baby snugly to her back and sat down
again to wait for her food. Though she was quite a long way
from him, he heard the rustle of her skirt like thick water stirred
by strong winds and he smelt the pungent, seductive smell of fat
and scent blended from the contact of flesh, ox-hide, and pul-
verized *impepo* flowers.

"Give the queens their dish," he ordered Mpisi. The youngest
queen fetched it, and Nabo Sicenga, as the oldest, was privi-
leged to cut up the huge joints into manageable pieces and divide them among her co-wives. What they could not consume
on the spot, each kept for a later occasion. Nabo Sicenga deliberately ate relatively little, and sent Sicenga to put the remain-
der into her cooking hut.

Only when every group was served did the prince settle down
to eat from his own finely carved dish. Delicately he lifted a
juicy cut between long-nailed thumb and forefinger and slid it
between strong white teeth. There was little talk; the pleasure of
eating was deep and sufficient unto itself.

It is possible that the children would have been the first to
finish had they had their portion cut up like the adults', but instead a single large joint went the whole circle and each child
took a bite. Totwa urged each in turn to hurry, but they all,
Lamtana in particular, took their time.

With the flavour of a savoury morsel still on her tongue,
Lamtana asked, "What would it be like to have enough meat
every day?"

Totwa giggled. "What a silly question. There would never be enough cattle for that."

"I wish we could see," yearned Sicenga.

"But if there were," persisted Lamtana, "would it taste so good?"

Totwa choked, trying to bite and reply at the same time, and when she had recovered Lamtana commented critically, "You are a glutton."

Totwa retorted, "I am not. My mouth is too small and my stomach too big, but your mouth is too big and your stomach too small."

"Quiet, children, and get on with the rejoicing," interrupted Nabo Sicenga.

Totwa looked down, but Lamtana pretended not to hear. She had simply stated a fact, and found it silly of Totwa and Nabo Sicenga to react. In Lamtana's opinion, Nabo Sicenga was always trying to make peace even when there was no need, and in doing so, of course, often created trouble. Though Nabo Lamtana made no comment, the expression on her chiselled face showed that she was indeed annoyed that anyone else should tell *her* child how to behave. Lamtana hated the bickering that ruffled life in the harem, and she knew that she was too often the cause. Her next mouthful gave her no pleasure, and when the meat came round again she passed it on without taking her bite.

"What now?" asked Totwa. "I'm the one who should be cross."

Lamtana dismissed her. "Then be cross. I'm not."

Sicenga pleaded silently with Totwa to let her be, and Totwa, who could never be cross for long, grinned back and said nothing.

The food was nearly finished. An occasional belch met a chorus of sympathetic encouragement. The mongrel dog noisily crunched the sucked-out bones strewn for him on the ground.

Inside the cattle byre the old, wise men started an ancient chant, and the stronger voices of the younger regiments joined:

> "*Djia djia.*
> The hut of spears
> Is empty.
> The birds are dead.
> To kill is chief.
> *Djia djia.*"

While they were singing, squatting replete on the ground, moving their hands to the deep rhythm, a man and two boys were seen approaching. As they drew near, the man began to shout the chief's praise song.

"It's Mputuya with Feka and Timba," announced Sicenga.

"I can see," said Lamtana.

"They are too late for the meat," commented Totwa.

"How do you know the pot is empty?"

"Do you know that it isn't?"

"Sing, children," admonished Nabo Sicenga.

Mputuya Zwane stopped with a last flourish of praise, and he raised in his hand a stick, an unusual stick of deepest black wood with a shiny silver knob at the end. He was a huge fellow with an appearance of strength somehow intensified by a scar that caught the light, running from temple to chin.

Mhau called, "Come here, Zwane!"

Bending respectfully, Mputuya came forward, having first laid down his stick so that he could approach his chief unarmed. When within easy speaking range, he squatted on the ground.

The prince, having greeted him warmly, enquired, "How is it in the hole at Goli?"

"It's heavy," boomed Mputuya, his voice equalling his size.

"Then why go?" Mpisi asked spitefully.

Mputuya scarcely bothered to look at him, but said, "If some of us didn't go, we would all die of hunger."

"What do you eat there?" queried Beta.

"Oh, there's enough food, though the money's little. We dig the gold, but the whites keep it."

"How are my people?" asked the chief, regally excluding foreigners from his interest, but showing the deepest concern for his own subjects.

Mputuya replied at length. He informed the chief of those who worked with him in the same mine, and of those whom he met in different homes in the townships on his day off. Some had been away from Swaziland only a few weeks, others for months, and others for years. Several had taken up with loose women in the town and showed no intention of returning to their families and responsibilities in the country.

"They are crocodiles," Mhau pronounced contemptuously, "who slide into the water when we who are men approach. They eat alone and have others to feed their families." At this Mputuya looked steadily at Mpisi and added deliberately, "But sometimes their brothers at home are also like crocodiles."

Mpisi appeared to be deeply engrossed in cleaning out an ear with a little stick. Everyone knew that Mputuya was referring to Mpisi's notorious neglect of Timba's invalid mother, wife of Mpisi's no-good brother. The whole burden of looking after her had fallen on Mputuya, her own brother, who had brought her and her son into his own village and cared for them both.

"How do the women behave in town now, my friend?" asked Mhau, tactfully changing to a subject of perennial interest.

Mputuya told several illuminating stories, and kept Mhau and the company well entertained. He was one of the few subjects who spoke to the chief without effort and as an equal, and the chief listened to him with pleasure.

They had been friends since childhood; together they had herded cattle, hunted field-mice, caught birds, and fought with sticks. When Mhau had inherited his father's position, Mputuya, son of a leading councillor, had decided to work in the mines. Mhau was desolate at the first departure, and had sacrificed a beast and prayed to his own ancestors to keep his friend safe.

He was also afraid that the city might change Mputuya, might even keep him forever. But his fears were unnecessary. Mputuya came home with new knowledge but undiminished loyalty. He had gone away many times since then, and, through the protection of the ancestors, had always come back safely. Once he was reported dead. A fall of rock. A tomb in the bowels of the earth. But somehow he pulled through, and the scar on his face was the only visible reminder of his ordeal. Throughout the years his friendship with Mhau had endured, and the chief loved and trusted him more than any other subject. Mputuya now wore trousers and shirts, and his wife was a Christian, and his son, Feka, had been taken from herding three years ago and was still attending school. In spite of all these differences Mhau trusted Mputuya.

Mhau would have liked to have gone on talking to his friend, but knew that it was not wise, or safe, to show too much favouritism in public. But before dismissing him, he sent for a bowl of beer and Mputuya drank deeply; then he called to the two boys to finish what remained. Having thanked the chief, Mputuya went to sit with his age group, and the boys with the lolling youngsters. Feka was tall and strong-looking like his father, and Timba, who was thin and lanky, walked admiringly behind him. Lamtana, too, followed Feka, with her clear dark-brown eyes, noticing how straight and sturdy were his legs in tight new khaki shorts.

The sun was falling and the feast was over. The praises of Mhau the Giver still echoed in the ears of the guests as they wandered along the narrow paths that veined the countryside, linking their smaller homesteads to the bigger homestead of the chief.

Mhau himself had returned to his own hut and the wives to their separate enclosures. His was the largest single hut, and the only one built of stone. In it he entertained special friends and the wives as he desired them. Now he was ready to relax, but before he could do so fully he had to make his nightly round of inspection. He would have liked to while away the time with Mputuya. Instead he looked with contempt at Mpisi, who always accompanied him and was sitting near the doorway waiting to serve his master. After a long silence Mhau said, "How is your brother's wife?"

"She is sick, *Nkosi,*" said Mpisi humbly, hiding his resentment at the deliberate way in which the chief always described the woman as "your brother's wife" and never as "Mputuya's sister." "People learn too much wickedness in the city," he continued craftily. "Our medicine men haven't cures for all their poisons."

"They are too often powerless against witches," agreed the prince sadly. He peered outside. "It is late. Give me my torch," he ordered. "It is time to inspect the village."

The children were already asleep, all but Lamtana. They had laid themselves down early, replete and satisfied. Totwa, curled complacently on her sleeping mat beside Sicenga, had chuckled, "Tonight I will dream well."

Sicenga had grunted drowsy assent. Lamtana, flat on her back with her eyes closed, said nothing. She was full, almost too full, yet her mind was wide awake. Behind her eyelids paraded a fantastic picture of herself; she wore a shining cloth of green and blue, and her arms were bright with bracelets. She was sitting in a motor car with Feka, and they were driving down the winding road to faraway Goli. She had her own image of the white man's greatest city, an image built from stories told by men who had returned. "Of course," she admitted to herself, "most of them are big lies made up by the men to impress us women," but from them had grown her creation. Myriads of torches glowing from huge huts of queer shapes, some built on top of others, close together. Women in the strangest dresses, with coloured objects on their heads and shoes like Miss Sibanze's, the teacher's, enclosing their feet. A tremendous noise

**19**

of shouting, clattering, whistling, singing, and hooting. So many cars that you closed your eyes to cross a street. She had her eyes squeezed tight to enjoy the blaze of vivid, moving lights.

And she thought for a moment that she was still dreaming when she heard Mpisi's voice exclaim, "*Nkosi*. Look!" Then she recognized her father's voice responding sharply, "What is it?"

"There, on the pinnacle of the girls' hut. A baboon. There."

She lay hardly daring to breathe.

Suddenly, louder and clearer than any of her imagined city's sounds, she thought she heard the eerie chatter of the most horrible creature in the world. The creature closest to man, and the greatest mockery of man. The witch's familiar. Lamtana clapped her hands over her ears as she imagined the ominous creature moving overhead.

"Are you sure it was that?" asked Mhau in a troubled voice.

"Yes, indeed. What else could it be? When you shone your torch it disappeared."

"I can only hope my torch forestalled its evil." Then the voices and the footsteps passed on.

Lamtana wriggled closer to Sicenga, but it was a long time before she fell asleep.

Mputuya, his son, Feka, and his sister's son, Timba, had been the last to leave the feast. Mhau had sent a handmaiden to tell them to wait and the mother of Sicenga had given Mputuya a portion of meat to take with him to the women of his home.

Timba carried the gift, carefully wrapped in green leaves and bound with grass. When he came to their homestead, he laid it like a devotion in the cooking hut of Mputuya's wife, Nabo Feka, who received it with such loud acclamations of delight and praises of Jesus that Timba's own mother in the hut next door hobbled to see what was happening, and together they gave Him thanks.

Nabo Feka belonged to the Holy Apostolic Church of Jesus in Zion, which inculcated into its members a firm faith in the curative effects of a white uniform, a green girdle, and the name of Jesus. Nabo Timba was not visibly a member. She was still trying other traditional remedies for the mysterious and terrible illness that had befallen her shortly after her husband's last visit to her. But it created no conflict in her to praise Jesus as well as the prince, and to seek the help of a church as well as of ancestors and medicine men. She was in fact thinking of joining Nabo Feka's church as a gesture of affection for her brother's wife rather than from fervour or faith in Holy Apostolic teaching. She was more at peace at Mputuya's than she had been for many years, and Timba, her only child, was happy herding Mputuya's cattle.

After her experience with Mpisi she was deeply appreciative of the treatment she received from Mputuya. True, she had some claim for maintenance from him since he, as her brother, had used her marriage cattle to obtain his own wife, Nabo Feka. But bitterly she knew that a legal obligation could be fulfilled willingly or unwillingly, with generous kindness or cruel reluctance, and never once had Mputuya or his wife made her feel unwanted. She was aware that in apportioning the meat, Nabo Feka cut for her the most tender piece, of which, however, she was able to eat only the tiniest morsel.

Mputuya observed with anxiety and deep pity how little she ate. She had been a strong, buxom maiden and now she looked scarcely human. A strong drive for revenge surged through him. He vowed that he would find that man, Mpisi's brother; he would seek him out through the streets and slums of the city, not to bring him back (he spat at the idea), but to destroy him as he had destroyed his woman, so that he, too, would never again be able to enjoy work in sunlight or gorge delicious meat. He, Mputuya, refrained from resorting to sorcery; he wanted to inflict revenge himself with his own powerful hands.

So dark were his thoughts that he did not at first hear his wife talking to him, but finally he noticed his sister's pleading eyes and he drew himself together.

"What is it?" he asked, excusing himself with "I am tired and my thoughts left me."

"I was telling you," repeated his wife, "about the new healer of our church who has come from Zululand."

"A healer?"

"Yes. A prophet. Blessed with the Holy Spirit." She recounted stories of wonders that the stranger had performed, emphasizing in particular the cures he had achieved in most desperate cases. He was staying for a while with a priest in the neighbouring district, and though she herself had not gone to hear him, many of her co-religionists had, and all agreed that he was indeed a prophet.

Mputuya listened without much sympathy. He had given up hope of his sister's cure; her body was tattooed with incisions made by different medicine men he had employed and paid. He had even suggested taking her to a white doctor at Mbabane Hospital, but she had protested that hers was not a sickness that white people—who did not believe in sorcery—could cure, and since in his heart he agreed, he had not persisted.

His wife, whose religion forbade the use of medicines other than holy ash and water, had previously suggested that a healer "prophet" of her church be brought to "lay hands" on the invalid. But Mputuya had little confidence in these strange men who wandered round the countryside in their white-and-green raiment, holding aloft magic rods and claiming to be possessed of the Holy Spirit. Who was this Holy Spirit, anyway, Mputuya asked himself, that could possess many different bodies all at once?

He put more trust in the traditional diviners inspired by deceased ancestors. Not that he trusted them entirely, either—too many were frauds trading on the credulity of fools who shouted "We agree" very loudly each time the diviner seemed to hit the mark in his diagnosis, and who dropped their voices to a dull monotone when he misfired. No, such impostors were not for him. He believed in diviners who did not rely on such easy clues, but were able to diagnose without a single word being spoken by the supplicants and without even seeing the patient. Such a one was the renowned Incabanga of Namahasha, an ugly little hunchback with many wives. It was from him that Mputuya had learned the nature of his sister's illness, and how it had been caused. That evil-doer, her husband, had injected it into her to prevent her bestowing her favours on any other man in his absence. Then he had abandoned her, without even removing his witchcraft.

Mputuya had not the heart to tell his sister the verdict pronounced for her by the wise Incabanga, and had gone on calling in different medicine men and herbalists. And when his wife was speaking he noticed that his sister was looking at him with such desperate sadness that he said, "All right, let us try this healer."

So very early the next morning he left with Feka to fetch the prophet. Timba was taking the cattle to the pasture, and on his way he met Sicenga, Lamtana, and Totwa, coming from the river where they had bathed.

"Why are you alone? Has Feka's school started again?" Lamtana asked.

"No, he has gone with his father."

"Where have they gone?"

"To fetch a new prophet who perhaps can help my mother."

The girls were full of sympathy and curiosity. They had heard of the prophet; his achievements and behaviour were part of local gossip.

"Can we see him?" asked Lamtana.

"Oh yes, Nabo Feka wants people to come and pray with him and has gone to call all her friends."

"We'll help pray," said Totwa.

"Yes," agreed Lamtana. "We will see each other later at your home."

The chief did not encourage preachers to come to his own homestead; not that he was discourteous if they arrived—on the contrary, he sent them food and let them sit as long as they felt inclined—but he himself remained occupied with affairs which, he would tell Mpisi to inform his guests, were "important." His wives, more anxious to please him and his ancestors than to win the grace of unknown gods, followed his example and remained aloof. But the children were permitted to listen to the varied visiting emissaries of Christianity.

On the whole they were amused rather than impressed, and after the visitor had gone, Totwa would entertain an appreciative audience by intoning a spate of meaningless words interspersed with impassioned calls of "Jesus," "Satan," and "Amen" and accompanied by exaggerated antics and grimaces. From all accounts, the prophet promised to be fun. The girls watched for him. Past noon they spied Mputuya and Feka returning, and with them was a strange figure dressed in a huge brimless hat topped by big white feathers. Over the body, reaching below the knees, flowed a white robe bound at the middle by a cord of vivid green, and from beneath the robe emerged a pair of purple trouser legs. Aloft in the air this "prophet"—for who else could it be?—held two snowy rods stripped of bark, one rod pointed and one twisted into a symbolic circle.

"He looks silly," giggled Sicenga.

"He's trying to look like a white man," announced Lamtana.

"Let's go now and hear him," pleaded Totwa, adding with a fearful thrill, "I hear he bites."

They could not resist this. They followed the path to Mputuya's home and stopped outside Nabo Timba's hut. From within came the sound of voices. Suddenly the prophet himself emerged. On seeing the girls he stood still, staring from wild eyes, then greeted them in a harsh sing-song voice; they responded a trifle nervously. They stood in graceful posture, their limbs glowing in the sunshine. He remained watching them silently for a few minutes, before he announced: "It is well done, God."

"I didn't hear you," said Sicenga politely.

He repeated gravely, "I said well done, God."

He gave a sudden high neigh and walked off abruptly, leaving the girls staring at each other, not sure whether they could allow themselves to laugh.

"His eyes frighten me," whispered Sicenga. "Should we go home?"

"No, I want to see what he does," replied Lamtana bravely. "I'm going inside. Come."

There were already five or six others, including a mother with a sick, whimpering child, in the hut. The girls sat close together on the women's side. Nabo Feka put a bowl of clean water and another of ash in the centre. The prophet returned, and other people trickled in. His eyes roved over those who had come to hear him. Mputuya was not present.

With a startling "Ha!" the prophet raised his arms high above the people, closed his eyes, and began to pray, invoking the Holy Spirit to drive out Satan and lead the wicked into the path of righteousness. His voice, which had been soft at the beginning, grew loud and nasal, he inhaled frequently, and he ended his short sermon with an enormous "Amen, Amen, Amen, Amen." The audience repeated the Amens.

"Now let us sing." He gave the words of his hymn: "The Spirit is everywhere, everywhere."

The company took up the words and melody. Over and over they sang the same line, their bodies responding rhythmically. Lamtana's eyes were fixed on the preacher, and it seemed to her that his body grew more than humanly tall and that his eyes were bright stars that shone from a high, dark firmament. As he stopped the first hymn with the Amen magic and began another chant, she whispered to Totwa, who sat wedged beside her, "He is a great person. I think God himself is like that."

They did not notice how late it was getting. Time was motionless under the spell of repetitive chanting in the hut thick with the heat and sweat of bodies.

The mother with the sick baby came forward beseechingly. The prophet seized it from her, held it high above his head in both hands, and shouted, "Out Satan." The baby screamed wildly. He brought it down almost to the ground, uttering peculiar noises that rose above the singing.

"Amen," he yelled, gripping it by an arm, and with his free hand he soused it with water, rubbed ash over its wriggling little brown body, gave it a violent slap with the words "Holy Ghost," and thrust the infant back to its anxious mother, who tried her best, but temporarily in vain, to quiet it.

Nabo Timba shuffled toward him and caught at his robe to draw his attention. He gazed at, and through, her. He neighed, threw back his head, his eyes wide open with whites gleaming. Sweat shone on his forehead. He pursed his lips and uttered high piercing sounds in the expectant, deep silence. He put his hands on her head and jerked out, "Go demons. God. The sick are here. Go. I banish you Satan, go. Help them Holy Spirit. Witches kill people. Let them believe. Holy Ghost in my hands. Worship. Worship. Behold the Lord. Holy Ghost see these women and children. Pity them. Go Satan."

As he continued, a terrible frenzy possessed him. He struck Nabo Timba fiercely on her back, shouting, "Get out Satan. Go demons."

He took the holy water and splashed it on her, and rubbed her wildly with the ash, while she sat trembling, submissive, with the anguish of fading hope in her eyes. He was babbling incoherently, but when the singing abated in vigour he yelled, "Amen, Amen," and the response came, "Amen, Amen, Amen, Amen." He shoved his way to where the girls sat huddled, and some of the women began crying and making hissing noises as their bodies pressed against each other, and the prophet pushed between them. Unable or unwilling to move, they submitted to his hands and continued to sing and shout. Foamy spittle started trickling from his mouth and mixed with his sweat, spattering the excited chorus. Possessed, he fell on his knees, heedless of the interwoven limbs, and reached toward the girls, uttering passionate cries.

Lamtana felt her whole body freeze as his face came close to hers. His eyes were mad. She wanted to scream with fear, but could only mouth "Amen."

It was at that stage that Mputuya squeezed into the hut. He watched the orgy with growing disquiet and disgust, then grabbed Feka, who was sitting beside him, and ordered, "Come outside."

They pushed through the low door and into the fresh, cool air. So rapt were the women, so engrossed in the antics of the prophet, that even Mputuya's own wife and sister, usually observant of his every movement, had not noticed his entry or his exit.

His eyes were blazing and his voice hoarse as he exclaimed, "He's a madman. We must drive him out."

Feka, reeling in the fresh air like one intoxicated, replied vaguely, "Amen."

"Shut up with Amen!" shouted his father brutally. "Fetch my stick."

Standing waiting outside the hut, he let forth a torrent of abuse and yelled at those within to be quiet, but no one heard or heeded. His face was taut, the scar looked like a raw wound, and his heart thundered through his head.

When Feka returned with the stick, Mputuya took it without a word and went back into the hut. At first all he could see in the dim light were twitching, writhing bodies, but soon he discerned the white robe and heard the prophet's voice screaming "Go out Satan" over the person, the familiar person, of Nabo Feka, his own wife.

Blind rage filled his heart, and he shouted in a voice terrible and broken, "Clear out! You, you Satan!"

But the prophet did not hear, and next second the headman's black stick with the silver knob beat down on the high brimless cap. The prophet crumpled like a bag. The stick shone and struck again. Women and children began rushing, screaming in panic, through the low door, clambering heedlessly over the prostrate body.

"Loose women! Animals!" Mputuya screamed in contempt as they fled from his reach.

The chief's children were pressed out of the doorway in the general stampede. Sobbing with fear and exhaustion, they stumbled outside. It was almost dark.

"What are you doing here?" Mputuya shouted at them. "Go home. You should not mix in this madness." They fled from him, speechless.

On the road Lamtana panted out between hard sobs, "He brought the madman to his home and then shouts at us." The others were too upset to speak.

Mpisi strode to meet the girls, demanding, "Where have you been? I was sent to find you."

Lamtana replied, "It is all right. We will explain to our mothers."

"They will kill you," he said with some satisfaction. "What will you explain?"

It was indeed difficult. When the mothers saw the girls they shouted angrily, "Where have you been?" and, before they could reply, began to scold and threaten them horribly.

"Forgive us," pleaded Sicenga.

When the deep maternal fears had spent themselves in loud abuse, Nabo Sicenga repeated, "Where have you been?"

Sicenga and Totwa hesitated, and Lamtana answered for them in a low voice, "We were caught at Mputuya's by the prophet."

"We escaped," breathed Sicenga.

"From what?" her mother asked. "Tell me."

Lamtana stumbled out, "The prophet that Mputuya brought for Nabo Timba. He laid hands on us and spat on us. We were forced to pray and sing. Then Mputuya killed him and blamed us."

"We only wanted to help pray for Nabo Timba," sobbed Totwa.

"Mputuya said he was Satan," said Sicenga. "We ran all the way home."

Though they tried to describe what had happened, they could not find words for the horror they had experienced. The mothers listened and concluded, "They have escaped."

Eventually the girls went to their own hut and stretched out their sleeping mats.

Sicenga asked, "Do you think Mputuya killed him?"

"I hope so," Lamtana replied fervently, adding fiercely, "I will never, never believe in prophets again."

She couldn't blot out the preacher's eyes, nor stop the sound "Amen, Amen" beating in her ears, nor forget Mputuya's fierce denunciation, "Loose women! Animals!" She went hot with shame. She remembered the baboon that had settled on the roof, and wondered who was responsible for all these misfortunes.

Early the next morning, Mputuya, accompanied by Feka, came to the chief's village. He walked heavily and scarcely returned the greetings he received. Lamtana saw him coming and deliberately avoided meeting him, but, from behind the entrance of her mother's reed fence, she tried to see what was happening.

Mpisi announced the arrival to the chief, and, knowing something of the events of the previous night, was curious to find out more. Afraid to ask directly, he followed them into the chief's hut and crouched unobtrusively in the far corner.

Mhau, who had received his report from Nabo Sicenga, his companion for the night, enquired coldly of Mputuya what it was that brought him out so early. Mhau's present concern was less for the children, who, after all, were safe, than for his own position. He was deeply disturbed that Mputuya had not consulted him before bringing the prophet to his home. In the past, not to inform a chief of the arrival of a foreigner, especially a medicine man of any kind, had been akin to treason, and though under the white man's law Mhau knew that he could inflict no punishment for this breach of custom, he still expected to be informed. If Mputuya, his friend, did not bother to take this precaution, what subject could he trust?

Mputuya, engrossed in his own anxiety, was quite unconscious of his negligence and of the chief's displeasure. To him, too, the orgy in the hut had become insignificant; a more real danger lay ahead, the terrible danger of a case in the white man's court. How badly was the prophet hurt? If he died, or if he recovered, what would be the sentence? The white man's laws were incalculable; for nothing they put a man in jail, for nothing they inflicted lashes. Good men were hanged and witches and prophets roamed freely. If the prophet laid a charge of assault—as he undoubtedly would if he could—what white man would understand that he, Mputuya, could have acted in no other way? Not for one moment did he regret striking the impostor; if the situation were repeated he would do the same again. As he described how he had brought down his stick, his large eyes, bloodshot from a sleepless night, shone like live coals.

"It is your luck," said Mpisi from his corner, "that you didn't kill him."

"It is his luck," shot back Mputuya, "that he wasn't killed."

"Is he badly hurt?" asked the chief, whose interest had at length been aroused.

"I don't know, but I think he will survive. He was saved by his cap!" He recollected broodingly, "When I left him in the hut last night, I did not care if he lived or died. But in the morning I went to see. He was alive, and I gave him water. If you agree, my chief, I will let him stay till he can walk again."

"So you come to ask me for permission now that the danger

is on you. Now you have a case before me as well as the white man. You, whom I trusted, brought in a humbug, a foreigner, who nearly killed my own children with his medicines. Had you come to me before, I might have saved you."

Only then did Mputuya realize that he had wounded his friend, and he exclaimed, "Forgive me, Chief. I did not mean to pass you by. My sister's illness pushed me outside my senses."

But Mhau would not let himself be won over immediately, and reproached his friend with an air of aggrieved dignity: "We grew up together. You know our law as well as I do. Why did you throw it aside? Have you changed, like others who follow only the white man's law or no law at all? I trusted you with my life; do you play with me?"

Mputuya urged him to believe that he had intended no disrespect, and definitely no disloyalty, and concluded his plea: "I wronged without thinking. Do with me as you wish."

The chief, realizing then that Mputuya was sufficiently convinced of the gravity of his neglect and humble enough to confess it fully, condoned the offence. He consoled him, saying, "The city makes us forget our customs. We become fools, caught in white man's laws." And to comfort him he continued, "Though you did wrong not to consult me, you did right to strike that sorcerer. If he reports you, we will try together to confuse him. Anyway, preachers are always cowards, shouting 'Peace' and 'Amen,' and I am sure we can work out a plan."

If it occurred to Mhau that the white administration expected him, as part of his chiefly duties, to report such cases, he dismissed the idea as absurd. He now wanted only to protect his friend, not to submit him to punishment by aliens.

At this critical point, an old man's voice was heard outside the door saying, "Wait there. I will announce you. Perhaps the chief is still sleeping," and through the low doorway crawled Beta, his little wizened face peering from his shell of an old army coat.

"What is it, Father?" asked Mhau impatiently. "I am not asleep. I have heavy work on hand."

"It is only a policeman," said the old one wryly.

"A policeman," Mhau repeated.

"Already," Mputuya said, sitting bolt upright, his eyes bulging. "How could a man who but a short while back was nearly dead have walked so many miles to the court-house?" It did not seem possible—yet, there was the policeman.

"What does he want?" asked the chief, more realistically.

"I don't know."

"Go, Mpisi, and tell him to wait at the council place. I do not have to run because he is a policeman."

Mpisi left and Beta squatted beside Feka, who had been listening to everything and suffering with his father.

Mputuya said to Mhau: "If he takes me, *Mntan'enkosi,* I beg you, help my orphans."

"I will not throw them away, my friend. Nor will I tell the police you are here. Stay till I return."

He walked weightily on his broad soles into the sunshine, where his councillors were lolling. When they saw him, they loyally shouted, "*Nkosi Dlamini.* You who are beautiful. You who are big." Mpisi spread for him a black goatskin rug on the ground, and he sat down and looked around. The policeman sat a little apart, straight and swanky, his gaitered legs conspicuously displayed. Mhau, keenly aware of this minion of white men, deliberately ignored his presence till Mpisi announced, "*Nkosi,* this policeman says he is sent by the government."

"Oh. That policeman. Call him."

The policeman shuffled nearer, his whole bearing a subtle combination of arrogance and deference. As a Zulu he was contemptuous of the Swazi, who, preferring peace to war, had hidden from their enemies in mountain caves and had had to be smoked out. Still, he had to concede that strategy paid; they had a country and a king, while his people had lost their country to the Boers and their king to the English. He greeted the prince humbly, and was graciously acknowledged.

"What brings you here?"

"This letter, *Nkosi*." From his jacket pocket he produced a large official envelope.

A letter. Mhau smiled with relief. A man was not arrested in a letter. Pleasantly he asked to know the contents of the envelope.

"They did not tell me, *Nkosi,* but I think it is about a meeting."

"Read it."

"I do not know how to read, *Nkosi*."

"A policeman should know." The chief felt smug as he continued genially, "When you bring a letter, you should know the message it carries or how to read it. You are a policeman, not a postman."

"You speak the truth, *Nkosi,*" applauded his audience. He turned to them.

"Who can read us this letter?"

They looked helplessly at him, and then he remembered that Mputuya's son went to school and he sent Mpisi to call him, referring to him as "my age-mate's son" and not as child of Mputuya, for the danger to his friend was not yet past.

Mputuya half-rose as Mpisi entered the hut, then, seeing who it was, sat down again, asking, "What is it?"

"Nothing. The chief wants your son."

"My son?"

"He wants him. Hurry, boy."

"Go, my child. You have done nothing."

"Yes, Father."

Feka obeyed and, ignorant of the reasons for his summons, was so terrified that he walked past Lamtana, who had slipped out to greet him, without even seeing her. Astonished and strangely disturbed, she stopped to watch him and saw him take the envelope from the policeman, turn it round, open it, and begin to read.

She could not hear what he said, but noted how attentively everyone listened to him, a mere boy, reading from a small piece of paper. "He is smarter than any of those old councillors," she thought with a thrill of excitement. "He knows writing. He knows even more than my father."

When he had folded up the message and put it back into the envelope, the chief said firmly to the policeman, "Next time, speak it. Now go back and tell the office chief that I have heard what he says and though I don't know what this meeting is about, because that he forgot to write, I will come."

Old Beta said sourly, "He did not forget to write down a time by the watch, and the day of the month. We must not be late, even if we don't know for what."

Mhau entirely agreed. Then, being the chief he was, he sent Mpisi for some beer to regale the policeman before sending him away.

Feka, conscious that his father would be awaiting his return with the greatest impatience, took the opportunity to leave by following Mpisi.

"Feka." This time Lamtana called him by name as he was about to pass her mother's hut.

He stopped and smiled at her.

"What did it say?"

He told her.

"You are clever," she said with such sincere admiration that he had to agree. "I, also, want to learn," she continued eagerly. "I, also, want to read and write. I want to know books. I want my head to open my eyes! Help me."

Slightly bewildered, he responded, "I will try, *Nkosatana.*"

"Then we will be clever together." She beamed, and ran back into her mother's enclosure. Her heart made a song: "I am happy. So happy. I am going to learn. I will be the wise princess."

Feka went on to his father.

Though it was cool, Mputuya's skin felt clammy. Unable to hear what was taking place outside, he heard frightening conversations inside his own head, ending with the refrain, "I sentence you to six months. I sentence you to five years. I sentence you for life." The sweat poured down his body. It was not the hard labour that he dreaded—breaking stones or making roads in the sunlight was easier than working deep under the ground—nor was it the treatment (which everyone who knew said was better in Swaziland under the British than in the Republic under the Boers), but prison killed the manhood. He had seen its effects on others, good men who, after a long sentence, came out with hard eyes and shorn heads and not a penny for all the time they had worked. It was better to fine a man, or even beat a man, than lock him up like a dog at night and make him work for nothing in the day. Why, he asked himself, why did the white man's law inflict that punishment? From what books did the judges read their judgements? One day perhaps Feka would read those books and explain those laws.

It was then that Feka came in, and Mputuya asked through cracked lips, "What is it? Where is the policeman?"

"He is going, Father. He only brought a letter about a meeting, and I had to read it."

"Was that it?"

"Yes, Father."

Mputuya put his hand over his face as relief loosened the coil of tortured thoughts. A nerve twitched behind the smooth scar. Feka sat, concerned and respectful.

When Mputuya spoke again it was with a quiet intensity, but the question he asked seemed quite unrelated to all that had happened. "My son, how are you getting on at school?"

Feka looked a little blank but answered, "I get on well, Father."

Mputuya nodded approval. He was struggling laboriously to express an idea that was developing in his mind, an idea he had never before considered. "You must go on learning. I see that the world is the white man's through his papers. We black people must get that knowledge that is written down. If we don't, the whites will always do with us as they wish. They will never show us their hearts, but their hearts are written in their books." He was thinking aloud, trying to clarify to himself and his son the idea that the release from tension had somehow triggered, the idea of the importance of knowledge.

He was interrupted in his intellectual struggle by the entry of Mpisi. "The chief says you can now go to the council."

They joined the men under the tree, and Mhau said, "We have been talking over your case, my age-mate."

"What have you to say?" queried Beta. "Tell us all."

Mputuya stood up, his face tightening with concentration as he tried to remember what he had said, seen, heard, and done since he returned from Goli and found his sister in so pitiful a condition, till his attack on the prophet.

When he had finished his story, the old men put their questions, unravelling the threads of kinship obligations that knit the events together. On those obligations, and not on any white man's law, they gave their verdict. The prophet was clearly the guilty party, and though Mputuya had committed a serious breach of tradition by acting independently of his chief, he had in all other respects behaved as an upright man, striving to fulfil his duties to his family and to protect them and others from a dangerous and immoral outsider.

"It is a terrible thing," lamented Beta, "that we can't punish him, but now it is the world of the whites and good men suffer through their bad laws."

"Perhaps," suggested Mpisi craftily, "Mputuya could hide himself from them. If he returned immediately to the town, he might escape them."

"I will not run away," replied Mputuya, and all the others supported him, angrily discounting Mpisi's plan.

After further discussion and suggestions, Mhau expressed the opinion of the council. "Mputuya must stay and fight his case. We will help him with witnesses. We will teach the prophet not to play with God and insult our ancestors."

*"Nkosi Dlamini,"* came the obedient chorus.

"Now go home and see what has happened to the villain, and if a policeman come to you, send your son to report at once."

Deeply grateful, Mputuya and Feka left. They walked silently and quickly, the man in front. He had come without his stick, and his hands hung loose and empty at his sides, dark folded wings moving on the ground.

Feka was involved in himself. He thought, "How strange that on the same day that my father told me to keep on with school, Lamtana, daughter of the chief, should say I was so clever and should want me to help her learn." He could not understand his father or the girl. He had gone to school at the instigation of his mother, who wanted him to be able to read from The Book, and he acquitted himself well because he was intelligent enough to appreciate that schooling was a privilege for which his father paid heavily. But he had not experienced any deep urge for learning; he lacked Lamtana's imagination and Mputuya's insight.

## 5 · THE MOTHERS AGREE

Lamtana wasted no time in telling her sisters of her desire to go to school. "And you," she stated with conviction, "should want to go, too."

"Why?" asked Totwa. "Our elders didn't, and they manage."

"The world is changing," Lamtana loftily quoted a frequently heard remark. "Now it is the world of white men's wonders. But," she added skilfully, "if you don't want to know them, stay at home."

"It might be fun," speculated Totwa.

"I can't see Teacher Sibanze giving us fun," said Sicenga, pulling a horrible face at the thought of the prim mistress in charge of the only school in the district.

"You don't have to stay if you don't like it," reasoned Lamtana.

"If you're so keen, why don't you go alone?" asked Totwa.

"I don't mind. It's your life. I just don't like you to waste it."

"I think you're thinking more about yourself," said Totwa shrewdly. "You know that the mothers might only agree if we all three asked together. Still," she said good-naturedly, "we'll help you. As you say, we can always run away from it."

Lamtana denied hotly that she was motivated by self-interest but admitted that their support might increase her chance.

So, without much enthusiasm, Sicenga and Totwa agreed that they would, if necessary, also go to school.

The three mothers were kneeling in the yard of the main hut preparing the evening meal, their strong arms moving back and forth to the monotonous beat of the grinding stones.

"Come and help us," said Nabo Lamtana.

Competently, the girls took over. After the meal, when they could all relax, Lamtana began with tactful formality: "Mothers, we have a request."

"Speak it," said Nabo Sicenga.

"We children know nothing. We must learn from you, our mothers. You have fed us and taught us, and now we are growing up, but we are worried and we ask you for help."

"Speak straight, now," said her mother.

"We see much that we don't understand." Lamtana repeated her arguments about how the world was changing and the wonders of the white people, and ended with the words, "We, too, want to learn books."

To support her, Totwa explained a little sadly, "It is a pity that books are only learnt in school," and Sicenga voiced equal regret.

Since none of the mothers had ever been to school, and in their immediate world they did not feel the need, the girls' request took them by surprise. They looked at each other suspiciously as though to say, "Who started all this?"

41

Nabo Sicenga remarked indulgently, "Our girls don't have to go to school. What can they learn there that will help them in the work of womanhood?"

Nabo Lamtana disagreed. This was partly perverseness—she seldom agreed with her co-wives—and partly because she herself was both intensely inquisitive and highly intelligent. Had she been born and educated in the different civilization of modern Western society, she could have been one of its intellectual lights, perhaps a leading scientist, probing, provocative. But, with her extraordinary beauty, coupled with both lust and vanity, she might have been left unfulfilled with the academic as her only role. The ideal setting for her brilliance and beauty would have been a circle in which she could be admired by leading statesmen and adored by artists of the world. As it was, she could only whet her mind on the edge of local gossip, and her beauty was confined to the limited attentions of a proud polygamist. No wonder her mouth looked disappointed and she had the reputation of being dangerously malicious. On the question of the school, she became vividly alive, a mature reflection of her daughter, Lamtana.

"The girls are absolutely right to want to learn," she stated. "At my home,"—the two co-wives exchanged commiserating glances at this all too familiar formula—"all the children are going to school. It is clear that schools are pushing the people forward, and our children should not be left behind with nothing but dust in their eyes. They must see what is written on paper as well."

Nabo Totwa, whose parents were squatters on a white man's farm, asserted, "I have never seen our Boer read anything but the Bible, and, as we aren't Boers or believers, what would our children read?"

And before Nabo Lamtana could reply, Nabo Sicenga complained, "I don't want my child to be a black white man."

"Who said they should become black whites or Boers? But I don't want them to be fools of the whites, either. The Bible is not the only book. Look at all the books in the office at Mbabane. Enough to fill this whole hut with trouble. Pass-books. Case-books. Cattle-books. Marriage-books. If you can't read, you put your thumb in ink like this,"—she demonstrated—"and before you know what you've done you've sold yourself to the white man."

Lamtana thought, "She is cleverer than the others. She will win for me."

But Nabo Sicenga continued. "Before, the world was good and people had respect. Though they had not learnt from books, they still were clever. By following white man's ways we have forgotten much that our elders knew. They lived till they were very old."

"Yes," added Nabo Totwa. "Today good people are killed by what is written in the books, and witches fly free."

Nabo Lamtana parried the thrust. "That is true, but white people aren't killed by our witchcraft. They know too much."

"How have our school people helped us, then? They learn only to cheat us better."

"We must learn, that we won't be cheated. It's not," she said judicially, "the learning that cheats, but the person."

Nabo Sicenga and Nabo Totwa realized they were being defeated but persisted with every argument they could muster until Lamtana, feeling the strain beyond endurance, pleaded, "Mothers, we want so much to learn." Loyally, but not vigorously, Sicenga and Totwa murmured support.

Nabo Sicenga consented grudgingly. "All right. You can go. You are still young enough for school not to matter."

Nabo Totwa commented somewhat irrelevantly, "If you want to sit in school for a year or two, you may. All the world is going by way of chairs. And look how uncomfortable that is!" Sitting bolt upright with her posterior perched in the air, she pushed an imaginary beret flat on her head with one hand and held an imaginary book close to her nose with the other in unmistakable caricature of the teacher, Miss Sibanze. Everyone laughed hilariously. In their home there was only one chair, a massive object with heavy wooden arms and coarse leather thongs across the seat, made for the chief, Mhau, by a student carpenter at a mission trade school, and produced with pride on the very occasional visits of white officials.

When their laughter had subsided, they turned to Nabo Lamtana for instruction.

"Now," she advised, "our prince must be told."

Nabo Totwa, who combined with her lighthearted gaiety a slightly cynical outlook, wondered to herself if Nabo Lamtana saw in her daughter's ambition some further power and privileges for herself, and said cautiously, "We will go together to speak to our husband."

"As you wish," tossed Nabo Lamtana, "though I would have thought it sufficient if one of us—Nabo Sicenga, or you, if you like—went alone. After all, he can't say no; he isn't a fool."

"Indeed he isn't," said Nabo Totwa indignantly.

"Come," intervened Nabo Sicenga, "let us all go together to him now," and she led the way.

Mhau, also, had never attended school, but four years ago, largely under Mputuya's influence, he had given the Wesleyans a plot of land not far from his friend's home, and there the missionaries had built a small schoolhouse. The first teacher was an unctuous young scallywag who, having seduced one of the pupils, was dismissed in disgrace by the white missionary when he came on his biennial visit. The present incumbent was Miss Emily Sibanze, of whom Nabo Lamtana hinted darkly, "She is clever—she has not yet shown her true nature."

Miss Sibanze kept her thin body shrouded in a long shapeless cotton dress, her hair hidden by a brown beret. The beret was particularly important to her, while what it covered intrigued the wives. Once when Miss Sibanze had arrived at the village, Nabo Totwa had been doing Nabo Lamtana's coiffure, poking up her high bun with a porcupine quill in traditional Swazi mode, and Nabo Totwa had asked the teacher what sort of hair she was hiding.

"It is braided," was the stiff reply.

"Show us," commanded Nabo Lamtana.

It was impossible to disobey, and there were revealed eight tight little plaits, each coiled in a square marked by a shining parting across the scalp. The wives, fascinated, had no shyness in examining each section, and it was indeed unfortunate that, while Miss Sibanze was still in her state of immodest exposure, the chief himself should have entered the yard. Acutely embarrassed, the teacher had squashed her beret back on her head, and ever after she had refused to remove it, even in strictly feminine company. The beret, together with the rest of her clothing, represented respectability and Christianity, and from this fortification she was able to look with some contempt on the married women in ox-skins, brazen girls in beads, and men in loincloths. The prerequisite for admission of pupils into her school—as into all mission schools—was "proper clothing," interpreted as dress and bloomers for girls, and shirt and trousers for boys. This qualification, the wives realized, would never be waived, even for children of the chief. Indeed, especially in their case, since Miss Sibanze was aware that the chief had looked on her, even in her state of undress, with disconcerting disinterest and patronage.

Mhau was not openly opposed to the school, but deep in his heart he mistrusted it. It stood for change, and change challenged his position. Yet he knew all too well that, however hard he tried, he could not stop change. His own king, the Lion of the Swazi, was full of school education. The old men, with whom Mhau agreed, criticized him for throwing away ancient customs and running after white men's ways. Mhau did not know, and would not have believed, that the white men said the king was not running fast enough.

When Nabo Sicenga, on behalf of the three mothers, spoke

about sending the girls to school, Mhau hesitated a while before replying. Slowly he pulled out the stopper of his carved horn snuff-box, tilted a little black powdered tobacco into the palm of his left hand, put back the stopper, delicately pinched up a little between the first and second finger, and sniffed it deeply, up first one nostril and then the other.

Finally he asked, "And where will you get the money to dress the girls for school?" indicating clearly that *he* had not the intention of providing it himself.

"We will brew for sale," said Nabo Lamtana promptly.

"Have you the grain to spare?" asked their husband.

"We will get it on credit from Simon, and if we buy the cloth at his shop his new wife will make it for us on the machine."

He realized that she had it all arranged. As his wives, wives of a chief, they could not go out to work for white men (the only ones with money), and for their possessions, few and perishable, there was no market. Their main crops, maize and millet, rotted if kept too long in the deep, flask-shaped grain pits dug in the cattle byre, so there was no point in hoarding or accumulating. If the harvest was particularly good, they would sell part of it to Simon, the trader, who would sell it back again when their stores ran low at roughly twice the price he had paid. Any money they got was quickly spent, again usually at Simon's, on candles, sugar, matches, paraffin, and salt—they all loved salt!—and there were always new and tempting luxuries, umbrellas, beads, glass bangles. If the wives could not pay, Simon would allow them *skewelet* (credit), carefully entered in an enormous ledger, and he very kindly did not press them, but let them redeem their debts over a reasonable period, aided by supplies of pumpkins, ground-nuts, and, more reluctantly, live chickens.

It was therefore natural that when they needed the clothing for their daughters they should think of approaching Simon for the grain required for the only economic venture that, if successful, brought in a clear profit—brewing beer for sale. Like all business enterprises, it carried an element of risk; if they brewed large quantities they stood to gain most, but if their customers had little money, or if the brewers gave too many free drinks to friends, they might lose even more than they had invested. The wives estimated that the material for the three basic uniforms would require at least one bag of corn (twenty shillings) and one bag of millet (twenty-five shillings).

They discussed exactly what goods they could bring to Simon, and how much he would offer, and Mhau, listening to the women, accepted that the decision to send the girls to school was really beyond his control and decided to grant his permission with grace and magnanimity. "I hear you, *Makosikati,* and they are your daughters. Since they are still green, I don't mind if they go, but see that they don't get spoilt. When they are ripe I will arrange their marriages without asking if their husbands can read books."

"*Nkosi,*" they chorused gratefully as they left him.

On their way out they noticed Mputuya and Feka coming up the pathway, and though they would have liked to learn the latest news, they were too polite to ask. Instead, they went to the main yard, where Lamtana was the only one of the girls waiting to hear the result of their interview.

"We will brew to clothe you," her mother informed her laconically.

Nabo Totwa, who was already beginning to have slight twinges of regret, remarked, "What a shame that dresses, which are so ugly, should eat up our credit."

"I have a chicken. Take it," said Lamtana spontaneously. "I'm sure Simon will give two shillings and sixpence for it."

"Do not waste your things," her mother said, so quickly that Nabo Totwa could not help laughing. Everyone knew that Nabo Lamtana was the wealthiest of all the women, the only one with cattle and goats of her own, given her by her father on marriage, but they also knew that she would never part with anything readily.

Lamtana, ashamed of her mother's meanness, said defensively, "It is my chicken and it is I who want to go to school."

"All right," shrugged her mother. "It is not mine."

"I will tell the others," said Lamtana, eager to be off.

Sicenga and Totwa received the news calmly, and when the little ones wailed that they would be lonely, Sicenga comforted them. "It will be for only a little while. I don't know if I'll go every day."

Lamtana was too elated to think of anyone else. From the top of the immense termite heap which was the recognized vantage point of the home, and near which the children were playing, she picked out the school in the distance, the sun pinpointing its unpainted corrugated-iron roof. Behind it stretched the broken line of hills, shadowed by dark gorges. The grass that had been fired in the winter showed vivid green between the stubble. Most of the indigenous trees had long since been cut for fire-wood, but here and there a wild begonia glowed with purple flowers and a twisted *umsinsi* sprouted red blooms from leafless branches. The homesteads, few and far between, merged with the peace of nature. Lamtana's eyes moved to the wind-break of blue-gums that marked Mputuya's home.

She longed to tell Feka that her parents had agreed, but could not bring herself to suggest to the girls that they walk past his father's home.

And it was Totwa who first mentioned Feka, asking Lamtana what she thought of his latest news of the prophet.

"What news?" she asked eagerly. "Has that chameleon left?"

"Don't you know?" asked Totwa, pleased for once to be ahead of Lamtana, and postponing a direct reply. "Didn't you see Feka? You were away such a long time that we were sure you were speaking to him and finding everything out."

"Did you speak to him?"

"No. He was with his father."

"So you don't know why they came here either?"

"Not from his mouth," Totwa tantalized her.

Sicenga interrupted this play. "I am sure it was to tell Father how the prophet left."

"We saw him go from where you are standing now. We watched him stumble along the road."

"How we laughed! His hat was quite flat, and he was using his rod as a walking stick! Like this." Totwa mimicked.

"I wonder if he's going to the court-house to complain. We might be called as witnesses." Lamtana thought for a moment and added slowly, "I would hate that."

"Don't worry. Father would not let us be taken." Sicenga had great faith in her father's powers.

Lamtana did not contradict her, but she had her doubts since she had seen the chief depend on a mere boy for the reading of a message calling him to the office of government.

Mputuya, whom Mpisi brought into the presence of the chief soon after the wives had left, was obviously less worried than on his last visit. He held his head high and again carried his stick, and when the chief asked, "Well, my friend, what have you done now?" he replied with a big smile, "I sent the lunatic away with Satan and the Holy Ghost."

The chief laughed loudly. "How did you do that?"

"When I got home from here, I went straight to his hut. He was sitting up, and I was glad. The boys took him food and he ate, but I did not speak to him, and he did not speak to me. This morning they again took him food. He ate and finished. Then he asked to see me; so I went in. We sat, and he asked me why I had struck him. I said, 'I do not like you to lay feeling

hands on my wife and my sister and the children of the chief!'
Then he asked me why, then, had I fetched him. I said I had
fetched him to cure my sister, but not like that. He said he was
doing what the Holy Ghost made him do. And I said I didn't
believe in his Holy Ghost. So he said I must have Satan in me. I
got angry and said, 'No, he is in you and so is his Holy Ghost,'
and I told him to clear out with the lot before I hit them all
again."

"Ha, ha, ha," applauded the chief.

"So," Mputuya concluded, "I saw that he was not badly hurt,
and that even if he reported me, I would escape lightly. That is
all, my chief."

Mhau, greatly relieved, warned him never again to have any
truck with foreigners. Old Beta joined them, and together they
talked over all that had happened and speculated on the
strangeness of modern times. When Mhau told them that his
three oldest daughters were going to school, Mputuya was ex-
tremely glad, but Beta was indignant. Mhau, who felt he had
to defend himself from any possible accusation of favouring
change, mourned the passing of ancient times, before the white
men owned the country, when the greatest honour of every man
was service in the regiment of the chief, not sitting on a bench
in a schoolroom run by a woman. Mputuya nodded, anxious not
to contradict his friend, who had been so loyal to him in his
danger.

He excused himself as soon as he could, after having agreed
to go with the chief to the meeting the following day, and returned to his home. He had much to attend to after an absence
of almost thirteen months. He always tried to arrange his labour contract so that he would be back in the country for the
ploughing season, but this year he had been delayed and by the
time he completed his "join" the first rains had already fallen.
He would have to hurry not to miss the main sowing, and there
were buildings which needed to be repaired and the fence of
the cattle byre that had been broken down, and implements

that needed reshafting. As he strode back from the chief's village, he thought gloomily of all this and wished he could have avoided wasting a day "listening to the wind of the commissioner."

Besides, he was tired. He would have liked to rest, and he thought enviously of some of his mates who, when they came home, did not bother about work, but basked in the sun and wandered from beer-drink to beer-drink. Young men they were, without responsibility, who could enjoy the excitement of the city. But the mines had no excitement for him. He needed the money and had no special skills. He needed money for many things, so he needed much money.

If only he had more land—one more large field. But that, too, was impossible; even his friend the chief, who allocated land, dared not take from another to give to him. There was no free land left, and the land he could use was already overworked. It had been his father's before him, and his father's grave in the old cattle byre was his beacon. He recalled the old homestead that had been moved after the period of mourning was over; the poles and lathes were carried separately, but the huts had been dug up as they stood and lifted out of the ground and raised on enormous staves on the shoulders of the men. Mputuya had smiled with pride that he, the new young headman, showed such strength that he could shoulder his burden more easily than any other. The traditional songs for moving the huts helped the other workers by their rhythm, but he didn't need songs that day; his body was full of music.

He had got good crops from the site of the old cattle byre until the land grew tired. It needed to rest, but where else could he plant? He would try it this one more year. He would plant it with maize, the new quick-ripening kind advised by the young agricultural officer with the long silky beard—Corn-Tassle, they called him. He was all right, he knew soils and crops; it was a pity he was as stupid—or obstinate—as all white men about livestock. Mputuya frowned at the recollection of the stupidity—or obstinacy—which, in spite of all Mputuya's efforts, would not let Corn-Tassle agree that it was wrong to tell the people to reduce the number of their cattle. To the white man they were pounds and shillings and pence, not *lobola* for a wife, not protection for a child, not inheritance to perpetuate the ancestral name and retain ancestral favour.

Mputuya valued cattle next to his son, his wife, and his sister. Each beast in his herd had its praises and history; he knew the subtle markings of their skins and the irregularities in the shape of their horns as well as he knew the outstanding features of his women; he remembered how often each cow had calved and the fate of the offspring; each new beast he bought was named after the mine at which he had sweated his substance for the money for its purchase; his cattle were the measures of his life, the tangible rewards of struggle. It was hard to part with them. At ploughing time he walked beside his team of sturdy oxen, skilfully flicking a plaited hide whip into sharp cracks of sound, and shouting masterfully to the animals to move on while his son pulled the team in a straight line and his wife followed behind and dropped the seed into the newly turned soil. He decided that he would look at seed at Simon's the following day on the way to the meeting, and if it was good, he would buy some for planting.

When he came to Mhau's home to accompany him to the meeting, the chief was still breakfasting off a bowl of frothy beer, but he was perfectly willing to stop at Simon's. Indeed, he himself needed new batteries for his torch and had thought of looking at new stocks of blankets that he heard had arrived.

While they were talking, Nabo Sicenga came to inform him that Nabo Lamtana and Nabo Totwa and their daughters planned to go that morning to the trader to buy the material for the school uniforms and have it sewn.

"I hear. Are you going with them?"

"No. I must work in my garden. Sicenga will go with me, but Lamtana wants to sell her chicken herself to Simon, and Totwa will help her."

He listened gravely, wondering where all this schooling would lead, but, having already committed himself, said magnanimously, "I will tell my white man to expect them."

Never did it occur to him, or to Mputuya, to wait for his wives and daughters, though all were going to the same shop, and if it had been suggested he would have been slightly shocked at the absurdity of such an idea.

Having finished the bowl, the two men rose. Mputuya was in old flannels and a khaki shirt, but his chief had dressed especially for the occasion, with a checked brown-and-white sports jacket held precariously by a single button over his usual clothing, and his *lijobo* resting on a new and very stiff red print. On his head, at a rakish angle, he balanced an enormous cowboy hat. As he walked off, with Mputuya behind, he was deliciously conscious of the admiration of his wives.

It was a clear and lovely day, with the freshness of new growth in the air, and it seemed but a short distance to Simon's shop. Quite a crowd of people were there, some to buy, others to look, and all prepared to gossip.

The shop consisted of a single room, rectangular in shape, with a bare plank floor and a high counter along the side opposite the entrance. Behind the counter were wooden shelves laden with blankets of vivid hues, cloths slightly less conspicuous, and a miscellaneous collection of groceries and haberdashery. In front of the counter on the right-hand side was what Simon called the hardware department—iron pots, hoes, chains for yokes, knives, and ploughs—and between were empty petrol drums filled with varieties of peas, beans, corn, and millet. To the left of the counter was a door leading to the office. Light and air came through the entrance and, once inside, were trapped, their only possible exit being backwards or sideways through a window, which, however, was always closed and seldom cleaned. If the heat, smell, and noise became overpowering, Simon would ask the onlookers to go outside, but he was a tolerant man, and instead of inconveniencing his customers, whom he regarded also as his guests, he preferred to remove himself for a short spell to his office, from which he would return undeniably refreshed.

Simon's red and wrinkled face was lit by a plump tippler's nose from which a net of purple veins spread to the puffed lids that swallowed up his twinkling little eyes. His hair, which had been dark and thick when first he arrived, was now a thin off-white circle, a narrow halo, around a bald pink dome. An open-necked grey shirt hung on his big-boned frame, and there was altogether something loose, or, rather, something not properly tied, about his whole person.

To describe him as dissolute would be too positive, to describe him as degenerate perhaps too harsh. Though he had lost interest in more respectable white settlers' society long before it had cast him out, he realized that to be accepted by the Swazi required qualities other than those of a bad white man. From them he wanted respect, as well as affection and tolerance, and in his heart he knew that this he had failed to achieve. As a result he was never completely at ease with them or himself. He was only a Somebody in a No Man's Land.

When the chief and Mputuya arrived, he was chatting with a little too much friendliness to a group of young dandies, but on seeing the distinguished customer he immediately walked over to him and offered suitable salutations in his rather high-pitched voice.

"*Nkosi,* I rejoice to see you." His Swazi was perfect. "Where are you going dressed up like that?"

"To the commissioner, my white man," replied the chief kindly, his poise and *savoir faire* contrasting sharply with the leaning-over-backwards bearing of the trader. "We have been called—though for what I don't know. Last time we went we heard fairy stories at midday. The government has put a child in the office. He should still be herding calves."

"Yes," agreed Simon, pulling in his loose lips to indicate that he, too, disapproved. "That is Tootles exactly. An interfering boy."

He turned to Mputuya, whom till then he had barely acknowledged, though he knew him well, and said with relish, "He has a lot of cheek in law cases, Mputuya, my friend. He'll punish you, all right."

Mputuya looked at him with disdain. Only a white man would broach so delicate a matter, one which in no way concerned him, without being asked for his opinion and with such unsympathetic directness. But all he said was, "So you have already heard of the case, Simon."

"Of course. Everyone was talking of it."

"What did they say?"

"That you killed him." And Simon proceeded to give a garbled account of the whole affair, to which the two men listened without much interest. Neither was prepared to discuss it with Simon; he knew too little and too much.

"Did you see the humbug?" was all the chief asked at the end.

"Yes. He passed here but he didn't stop. He was going as straight as he could to the office."

"Let him go. Him and his lies," said Mputuya, fingering his stick.

Simon changed the subject. "Is there something you are wanting in the shop?" The chief explained their business and was shown what they required. Mputuya agreed to buy half a bag of ninety-day seed corn, and Simon insisted on giving the chief two batteries for his precious torch.

Before allowing Mhau and Mputuya to depart, Simon invited them to his office to rest, carefully closing the door after them. In the office were two chairs, a swivel desk chair and a large arm-chair, facing each other across a desk littered with scraps of paper and chewed pencils; within arm's reach of the swivel chair stood a padlocked cupboard, otherwise innocent-looking. Facing the cupboard, in a heavy wooden frame, was a large coloured lithograph of King George V standing at attention.

The chief sat upright on the arm-chair and Mputuya squatted naturally on the floor while Simon, in the swivel chair, took a bunch of keys from his pocket, swung round towards the cupboard, unlocked it, and produced with a magician's flourish a bottle of brandy and, after a moment's hesitation, two finger-printed tumblers that he placed on his desk, which served conveniently also as a table. He filled the tumblers to the brim, graciously handed one to the chief, and kept the other for himself. Lifting his glass to eye level, he toasted his guest, the prince: "A good journey to the office." He swallowed his drink in one gulp, and the chief followed his example. The noble face remained immobile, the eyes closed for a second only, and he commented approvingly, loyally, "It has strength. Rightly do we call it Tears of the King of England!"

"Have another," said Simon, first refilling his own glass.

Mhau did not refuse but, having taken a sip, passed his glass to Mputuya, explaining with great courtesy that he had previously drunk much beer and feared that if he mixed it with more Tears he would have trouble with his stomach.

Mputuya swallowed slowly, with a connoisseur's pleasure, and, when the last drop disappeared, expressed a subject's gratitude and hopes for similar benefits in the future. Simon responded generously by pouring out two more tumblerfuls.

After several more minutes spent pleasantly in talking of crops and the price of cloths and cattle, Mhau asked what time Simon's watch said. On learning that it was nearly ten, he considered that, since the meeting was about to start, he and his friend had better be on their way, but promised to drop in again on their return to collect their purchases and gifts.

As Simon opened the door and they went back into the shop,

the chief noticed immediately the beautiful Nabo Totwa standing with Nabo Lamtana and the two girls, and he remembered that he had forgotten to tell Simon of their proposed visit. However, they appeared well able to negotiate their buying without his assistance. In front of them were rolls of printed cloth, which Simon's assistant was unwinding with admirable patience. In the corner nearby, Mhau also noticed the beady eye of a familiar bird, its legs bound firmly with grass.

The wives, who had, of course, already heard that their husband was closeted in the office with the trader, were made conscious of his presence by the chorus of *"Nkosi"* which greeted his emergence. They did not, however, turn to look at him, and he, equally sensitive, walked past with the benign remark, "Good, *Makosikati,* buy well. It is a pity things are so dear." Still without facing him, they agreed, "Exactly, *Nkosi.* You say the truth."

Mhau left the shop with a feeling of regret, and the road from Simon's to the meeting place seemed very much farther than from his home to the shop, though he knew that in steps it was not so.

Once the chief no longer needed him, Simon turned his attention to the wives, sending his assistant to serve lesser fry. After unrolling the material and pinching it for texture and pulling it for strength, Nabo Lamtana made the choice. They had no idea how much would be required, and so it could not be cut until they had consulted the expert, Mrs. Simon.

Mr. Simon was sure he had a way with women and never understood why his first wife, for whom he had given twelve head of cattle, ran off with a "raw Swazi," whose most conspicuous possessions were a mop of long hair like a gollywog's and a big open grin. Her father, being an honourable man, tried to force her to return, but this was contrary to Mr. Simon's principles and he insisted on getting his cattle back instead.

The only possible explanation of her conduct appeared to him to be that he had not yet made her with child, and when after a short period he gave bride-wealth for a new wife, he took care not to repeat his shortcoming. The girl, who was in all ways lovely, was appropriately named Lomusa (Kindness).

When Simon knew that she was pregnant, he experienced unexpected pride and joy, and he developed towards her the deepest affection, which she reciprocated with passion. He taught her to say in English, "I love you, my husband." Their happiness lasted but a little while. In the eighth month, late one night, she began to bleed. He carried her in his arms to the car and drove at fifty miles an hour over the winding, bumpy road to the hospital at Mbabane. He hooted loudly, and to the nurse in charge, who came from within, he muttered thickly, "My wife is dying."

She stared at him from a flat, white face, then turned her back on him and told an orderly to bring the girl in.

At the door of the theatre, he was told to wait. The dying girl looked at him and said clearly, "I love you, my husband," and he sobbed, "I love you, my wife." She tried to smile at him, and he broke down completely.

The nurse said with sudden compassion, "Don't give up hope."

When she came to tell him that his wife had died, he rushed wildly into his car and drove like a madman to his home. For two days and two nights he shut himself up in his office, and came out with eyes swollen from weeping and drinking. At the mention of her name he wept again unrestrainedly, unashamed for once of genuine emotion. For many years after that he lived alone, wedded only to the Tears of the King of England. Then he returned from a short holiday to Barberton—a little Transvaal town across the Swaziland border—with a third wife and a sewing machine.

The wife was quite plain, wore European dress, had learned English at a mission school, had trained as a hospital nurse, and did not touch any alcohol. The machine was a Singer, new and guaranteed. Simon was determined to prevent any repetition of his previous marital misfortunes; to guard against being made a cuckold he would not allow his wife to work in the fields or wander freely to different homesteads, and to satisfy her maternal instincts he encouraged her to sew dresses for the converts and the school children. He addressed her always by her name, Gladys. For business purposes he referred to her as "Mrs. Simon." In the company of Europeans he described her merely as "my housekeeper."

Mrs. Simon seemed satisfied with the arrangement. She sat most of the day at her machine in the front room of the two-room bungalow, which Mr. Simon could watch from behind the shop counter, looking through the open door. He was delighted when Nabo Lamtana told him that the wives of the chief wanted Mrs. Simon to make school dresses for their children, and he escorted them to the house. Nabo Totwa and, particularly, Nabo Lamtana were frequent customers at the shop, and with them he was on terms of easy familiarity, but the girls came on rare occasions and were only beginning to be interesting. His attention had first been drawn to Lamtana on the previous visit, when her mother had bought her the bracelets that shone so gaily against the clear young skin. Then, as now, something about the child—for he regarded her as such—reminded him of Lomusa, the wife he had loved and lost so tragically.

"Come back when you have been measured," he said in his friendliest voice, using the plural "you" but keeping his eye on Lamtana, "and I will give you sweets."

"*Nkosi*," they all agreed appreciatively.

"I have a chicken to sell, too," Lamtana informed him proudly. "I left it in the corner till I return. It's a beautiful bird. I want a lot of money for it."

"We will see," he chuckled indulgently. At the door of Mrs. Simon's workroom he left them and slouched back to the shop.

Mrs. Simon's table was covered with yards of fluffy white net and lace, and her small mouth was full of pins. On seeing her visitors, she deftly removed the pins and stuck them one by one into a pig-shaped pincushion. Her plain but not unattractive little face smiled a warm welcome, and she came forward with birdlike steps to bring the new customers into her sanctuary. At her insistent invitation, the queens sat gingerly on the edges of two chairs while she showed them the gown she was sewing—a wedding dress for a Christian—and she laughed kindly when Lamtana exclaimed, "I wish our school dresses could be like that!"

Nabo Lamtana then announced the purpose of their call.

Never had Mrs. Simon had such exacting customers. They looked through every single picture and pattern that, having rashly boasted of possessing them in the first thrill of royal customers, she had been prevailed upon to produce and, if necessary, unfold. Bought over several years at jumble sales in Barberton, they included torn packets of McCall's, Vogue, and Simplicity patterns and vast stacks of outdated women's weeklies and *Ladies' Home Journals*. Lamtana's first choice was a skin-tight gown cut low at the throat and back, reaching to the ground, and she strongly objected to Totwa's preference for a frolicsome creation of tulle. After considerable discussion, all regretfully agreed that those styles might not be altogether suitable for Miss Sibanze's school, and they began to choose again. Their next choice, "tailored sportswear for the hunt," was abandoned only when Mrs. Simon stated positively that it would be uncomfortable for ordinary sitting. Finally they decided, a little dubiously, to leave the "cut" to her, and she guaranteed that she would pick something both suitable and original. (In this way, too, she settled any difference of opinion between the sisters, for it was taken for granted that all three, being sisters, would appear in the same dress.)

Having decided in this way to leave the style to Mrs. Simon, they all went back again to the shop to see if the material previously selected would be suitable. The rolls were again brought down and spread out on the counter, and the process of pulling and pinching was repeated. They changed the original cotton, a turquoise blue decorated with a black bird design, for a dazzling chintz of royal purple with crimson and cream flowers growing in exotic shapes. Mrs. Simon decided that, with careful cutting, she could manage on two yards each. Two yards, at four shillings and sixpence, times three. The combined efforts of Mr. and Mrs. Simon gave them the total of twenty-seven shillings.

To make a profit of twenty-seven shillings, they decided they would have to brew one bag of corn (seventeen shillings and sixpence) and one of millet (twenty-two shillings and sixpence) and so sell sixty-seven shillings' worth of beer, cash.

"It is too much money," exclaimed Nabo Totwa; her soft round face grew serious and her eyes opened wide with surprise.

"We will succeed," said Nabo Lamtana with finality.

Lamtana proffered her chicken. It squawked and fluttered as Simon lifted it up and down for a few minutes in critical balance, then offered one shilling and sixpence. The entire family protested.

Nabo Lamtana put the top price. "It's worth three shillings, but give us two shillings and sixpence."

"What! This isn't a goat." Then, scornfully, "Two shillings and sixpence for a bunch of feathers like that."

"It's a beautiful fat bird." Lamtana challenged him, "You want to cheat us, White Man."

"*Hau.* Princess. How can you say that to me? Look, I don't like buying chickens. I only take them to please you people. I have too many, already, doing nothing but running around making a mess."

"They lay the eggs that you eat every day," she retorted angrily.

Her mother said haughtily, "If we want to *buy* a chicken, you ask three shillings for an old cock, but if we want to *sell* a chicken, a good laying hen, full of eggs, you offer one shilling and sixpence. Take it back, my child."

"All right. I'll give you one shilling and ninepence."

"No. That threepence more is not enough to help us."

"Please, Simon," Lamtana coaxed him, "two shillings and sixpence. Let me show you how fat it is."

He looked at her. "Two shillings and threepence and not a penny more, and that big money is not because the bird is worth that much, but because I want to help the children of the chief." So the bird changed hands. Lamtana parted with it sadly and for comfort chewed hard on the sweets Simon had given them as bonus. These sweets, with which he always crowned successful business negotiations, were very popular. They were in several colours, shaped like hearts, and printed with Zulu words which he read aloud and translated to mean "I love you." To the royal party he had presented a whole fistful.

Simon suggested that he divide the grain into four small bags for the women to carry home, but Nabo Lamtana decided the loads would be too heavy—for the others, of course!—and proposed that Simon ask the chief to send Mpisi or one of the lads in the barracks to fetch it by sledge on the morrow.

They were about to leave when Mrs. Simon remembered that in her excitement she had omitted to take the girls' measurements, so back they trooped to the sewing room for this last operation, which caused considerable boisterous hilarity, and for which the wives also willingly offered themselves. Since Sicenga was not there, they tried with words and gestures to describe her proportions, and Mrs. Simon promised to do her best. As she was very busy completing the wedding outfit—two dresses for the bride alone, and dresses for two bridesmaids, two flower girls, and two pages, in addition to the white wedding gown—she could not have all the uniforms ready for about two weeks.

From behind the counter Simon watched them say good-bye. The folds of his face sagged, and his Adam's-apple jerked as he swallowed. What was it about the girl Lamtana that made him think so poignantly of his beloved Lomusa?

The meeting had already begun when Mhau and Mputuya arrived. Not in the least apologetic, they stood for a few minutes taking stock before deciding where to sit. The only chair was reserved for Mr. Tootles, who at the moment was standing in front of it addressing a crowd of men squatting on the ground in front of him. Behind the chair was the flag-post, flying the Union Jack. On the left of Mr. Tootles stood the same policeman who had brought the message of the meeting, and on his right, also in policeman's uniform, the interpreter, a tall, very black man with a big voice.

The chief's arrival created a slight disturbance. Many heads turned towards him, and loudly murmured greetings of *"Nkosi"* interrupted the young assistant commissioner, who shouted,

"Why can't you Swazi be on time?" This was duly relayed back but none volunteered a reason, and Mhau courteously returned the greetings he received.

"Sit down," ordered Mr. Tootles. "I am speaking."

"The chief says sit down. He says he is speaking," came his enlarged echo. A few men nodded encouragement. Mhau, seeing an empty space beside old Beta, who had come in earlier, walked up slowly, followed by Mputuya. The interpreter conveyed to Mr. Tootles in an audible whisper that the late arrival was Chief Mhau himself, and Mr. Tootles, imbued with the discipline of bureaucracy, waited, albeit with ill-concealed impatience, for the chief to sit down.

Mr. Tootles felt, and looked, a little out of place. He seemed a conspicuously bleached young man, with pale-blue eyes and corn-coloured lashes, eyebrows, and downy hair, all of which merged softly with light-pink skin. He was only twenty-five, and very conscious of being "the only white man" amongst an assembly of "blacks." In his two years' service he had so often been told that "they" were children, he was afraid to recognize "them" as adults; in his official position he saw himself as their father, whose duty it was to instruct and, if necessary, punish. Mr. Tootles was himself unmarried; indeed, he was totally inexperienced. Punctuality was, to date, his passion; his only bedfellow and constant companion was a big gold watch inherited from his father, a teller in a small bank.

When the chief was comfortably settled, Mr. Tootles continued his address with the remark that he was glad to see so many chiefs and headmen present, and would enquire into the reasons why the others who had been called were absent. "Government"—spoken in capitals—"does not call for nothing. It deals with important matters, and expects the chiefs to show themselves worthy of trust and responsibility. There are several items for today's meeting, and when I have heard your opinions, I want you to go back to your people to tell them of Government's decision. The first thing is this recording of marriages. As you know, every chief has a book in which he has been told by Government to write down the names of every couple married in his area, together with the names of their parents or guardians, and the number of cattle paid and promised. This to me seems a very simple matter—and yet there are many chiefs who have not a single entry in their registers. Are there no marriages taking place? Or are the chiefs neglecting their duty?" Throughout this part of the address, the interpreter struggled with moderate competence and considerable volume. The chiefs remained unmoved. In different words, but with the same effect, Mr. Tootles repeated the first major message of "Government." He then went on to "Item Number Two, which is related to Item Number One," which the interpreter, hesitating for but a moment, announced as "the chief is going to go on speaking."

"The registers will help us in the matter of forced marriages," pronounced Tootles, again in a tone designed to inspire reverence and awe. "Government will not allow, I repeat, will not allow, forced marriages. Time and again this has been said, by others and by myself. Yet in the two years that I have been here three cases have come to my notice, in which fathers have tried to marry their daughters to men they did not love. In the last case, the girl ran to me for protection." (Sir Galahad was ne'er more nobly inspired and his weapons ne'er as pure.) "I called both the father and the villain he had chosen as son-in-law to my office, and warned them that if they touched the girl I would send them to prison for assault."

There was a sharp, horrified intake of breath, but Mr. Tootles, completely oblivious of the fact that his audience considered the girl had committed the most flagrant crime by reporting to the enemy camp a man who had most likely acted entirely in her interests, continued heroically, "Such cases must stop. Government will not permit it. No woman should be married without her consent, against her inclinations, to a man she does not love. To make her do this is a crime in the eyes of

Government and"—divine afterthought—"God. It is the duty of
you chiefs to see that such things do not happen, and if they do,
to report such instances to me."

Some of the chiefs were muttering vigorously, but Mr.
Tootles continued unabated, "You people must realize that a
woman is not a chattel, not a slave, to be bought and sold to the
highest bidder." His face grew a deeper pink with emotion.
"Among civilized people, men protect and cherish their women.
To force a woman, a girl, is—damnable." He exploded the
word. "Therefore, I warn you, this thing has got to stop. I will
now give you a chance to speak, but, as time is important, you
must be brief. I have more to say later."

The interpreter issued this decree, and Mr. Tootles sat down,
looked at his watch, and leaned back in his chair with a feeling
of mild self-gratification at his own eloquence and some regret
that he alone had been able to appreciate it to the fullest. He
wished that some of the other fellows, particularly the old district commissioners, had been present; then they would have
realized the stuff he was made of. They thought they knew everything simply because they could talk the lingo and knew a
couple of the customs, but times were changing. These chiefs
had to be kept in their places; they were not bad fellows—just
children, bullies perhaps, and needed firm handling.

Old Beta was the first to speak, looking more than ever like
an ancient tortoise as he poked forward his lined face crowned
with the waxen head-ring. He said, "Nkosi, it is sweet to hear
the words of those who rule us, so that we know we are not
forgotten. When we are summoned to the office, we tremble,
like children afraid of having done wrong without knowing what
has angered their father."

Mr. Tootles' pale eyes beamed, and the speaker continued
glibly and with apparent innocence. "We listen to your words and
search our hearts for our sin. I am an old man among my
people, and I have grown old in their customs, but when I
confront you, you see I am a fool, an old fool." The old voice

hardened subtly. "So I say in my foolishness that to me and my people, arranged marriage is a good custom, and if a girl is promised in marriage, she must not shame her father by refusing his choice and making him return the cattle given by the man to feed her till she is ripe for marriage. It is the custom of our ancestors, and we do not want to change it. Without arranged marriages there would be many women without husbands and many children without fathers. Therefore, to us the custom is good, and if the books will stop that custom, I think we chiefs should forget the books and keep to the custom. That is all I have to say since the chief does not wish to listen to long words."

As soon as he had sat down, another old man stood up. He was all skin and bones, with one drooping eyelid that gave a mocking, Puck-like expression to his face. He limited himself to a number of rhetorical questions. "What is this that the white man says? Why should we not look after our daughters by marrying them to men whom we choose and trust? What is this nonsense that says a woman can run to the white man's laws with her complaints? Is she not a child that her own father must protect? What need to write a few things in a book—when what is spoken around the things is more important?" He shot his questions at a rapid rate and high pitch of intensity with which the interpreter did not attempt to keep pace. When he had finished, someone from the audience shouted, "A man, indeed! Answer his questions." To which the interpreter, without first translating, replied, "Be quiet."

"What was that?" asked Mr. Tootles.

"Nothing, *Nkosi,* that man was just making a noise."

Lubelo, a thick-set, ugly man with a pock-marked face, stood up, his voice heavily ingratiating. *"Nkosi,* all that you say, we like to hear. We are in darkness and beg for light. We are but children and know nothing. Therefore, we accept your words with praise. The Lord bless you."

Mhau looked at Lubelo with unconcealed dislike. Unfortunately, he was the oldest son of Mhau's father's younger brother, and as such also an important member of the chief's family council. When Lubelo sat down, old Beta said contemptuously to Mhau, "His head does not take well. His words are hemp smoke."

After a few others had spoken, Mr. Tootles looked again at his watch. "Time is running out. Let the speakers keep to the point."

Mputuya rose, his huge body towering over the crowd. "Chief of Government and Chiefs of the Swazi, I am glad to be here, but what I say will not please you." Mr. Tootles glanced up at the interpreter in surprise.

"You, *Nkosi*—" he addressed the young assistant commissioner directly—"you will say I speak like a Kaffir." He used the term of contempt without embarrassment. "And you," he said, not flinching before the stares of ancient chiefs, "you will say I speak like a black white man. I have never forgotten that I am black, though I have spent more time working for the whites than living with my own people. I have never forgotten, because I am a man. I have a home, a wife and children to feed. I, myself, am not a buck to be hunted as food, nor am I a mole, to hide myself in the ground. But can I live like a man? Can we blacks live like men? The whites stopped that life when they stole our land. They killed us. They did not kill us with guns, but with papers. They gave our king, Mbandzeni, horses and guns and money and called him King, then they said, 'Put your mark on these papers, King, to show we are your people.' We were fools. We were asleep. And when we woke up, our king was without his land, and we were the white men's servants. A king does not sell his country; only white men buy and sell it with papers. We were deceived with papers."

These words, sombrely spoken, made the men look at Mr. Tootles with increased suspicion. The concessions, deeply engraved in memory and tradition, were a constant source of bitterness.

Mr. Tootles, who had no intention of allowing the meeting to take up so irrelevant an issue, interrupted, "Let him come to the point."

Mputuya ignored this reminder and continued. "As long as men have no land, and are driven from their homes to work, and even while they work they know there is still hunger in their homes, it does not matter what new laws are made, nor what old laws are broken. Whether we try to follow our custom of arranged marriages or accept the white man's way of letting women make love where they please is not the matter to break our heads about. When there are too many men in the city and too many women in the country, the men will take anybody's woman in the city and women in the country will go where their hearts push them. The old paths are closed, and the new ones cut for us by whites lead to confusion. Then we listen to lying prophets and shout Amen. We must not listen to them. We must find our own new road, and look for the truth in ourselves."

He was speaking with compelling concentration, the scar on his face gleaming silver-white as the sun caught beads of sweat which had collected there in a strange, immobile line. He ended his argument. "The road the white men made for themselves was by papers. Concessions. Taxes. Passes. Now marriage-books. The white man's power is in papers. We must get that power."

As he sat down, someone shouted, "Well spoken, Zwane," but others began to criticize and argue. They had listened with varying degrees of interest and comprehension. To most, each particular statement was clear enough, but not the argument as a whole. They attributed their troubles in a general way to the greed of the whites, but did not work through to the full effects, nor to any particular solutions. They knew they could not, even if they wished, drive the whites out by force and that the Ngwenyama, Lion of the Swazi, had failed to win back their land, though he had crossed the perilous waters to plead their case before the Great King of England. Most of his Swazi subjects believed that the greatest power of the whites lay in money, with which everything could be bought, even people. Old Beta had a theory that all money was controlled by the King of England in person and distributed downwards through the Resident Commissioner, District Commissioner, and other "chiefs of office," who allocated a certain amount to traders and employers who gave some back as "tax" and "profit," words which Mr. Simon had once tried to explain to Beta. The redistribution of money in such a way as to give Africans a larger share of the total was therefore blocked at the top, that is, by the King of England. Some of the young men from the city who heard this theory had laughed and said that money was controlled by quite a different set of people, and Africans could get hold of it through trade unions and strikes. Beta had been sceptical, but Mputuya seemed to agree with them, and now here he was, putting up all this story of paper bullets. Did he really believe that white men would ever let blacks get the real secrets? A powerful magician would never reveal his medicines to a rival.

The hubbub evoked by Mputuya's long harangue took Mr. Tootles by surprise. He had been steadily losing patience. His interpreter, interested in listening himself, had stopped trying to convey the meaning and shouted brief, disconnected sentences, which Mr. Tootles soon did not attempt to follow. Still, it didn't really matter. There was only a limited amount of time, and no one ever offered anything really practical. It was good to let them have their say without making too many interruptions, especially in the case of a fanatic like this enormous fellow. Obviously a bit crazy, but he couldn't be allowed to rant forever.

Tootles manfully cleared his throat and intervened. "Quiet. You must address the meeting, not each other. There is a little time left for one more speaker."

The men turned to Mhau. Deliberately, yet without any awkward or pompous mannerism, and with frequent pauses for the interpreter to translate, he stated what he understood to be the opinion of the majority. "*Nkosi,* we thank you for listening to us. We, too, have listened to you. But we do not like the words that you have spoken. They are hard words, words like stones. I tell the truth, white men are clever, they can read and write, they have motor cars and trains, and they can make night look like day with torches that go on and off. These things I have seen with my own eyes. But their kindness and their laws are not so clear."

Mr. Tootles again consulted his watch. "We have heard this before, and as it is now past twelve o'clock the speaker must finish."

The interpreter translated, a trifle apologetically.

"I hear him. Tell him to listen," said Mhau urbanely. "Tell him that the white man hunts with a gun and shoots the lion when it is still far away. But we who hunt with the spear must choose our path more carefully and creep in silence close to our prey. It takes a long time, but the end is the same." He put his finger to his nose in a cautionary sort of way.

"It is easy to look at the customs of others and say, 'That is bad'; if it is different from one's own it is not easy to say, 'That is good.' Therefore I say, let the white man keep the customs which he thinks are good, and let us follow the customs which our fathers praised."

He then explained why, in his eyes, arranged marriages were good and proper, and how, when there were several wives of the same man, the woman whose marriage had been arranged held the highest status, and her son was recognized the main heir. He stated that force was necessary only if the women were stupid and obstinate; most fathers chose men who would be reliable as husbands, not those who offered most cattle. "Only men who have been too much with whites think of selling their daughters to the highest bidder. In the old days," he said nostalgically, "no girl refused to obey her father, but now"—into his voice crept a note of despair—"it is the world of the whites. They say our girls must be free when they grow up. Free to spoil themselves."

Mr. Tootles protested with some irritation, "He's talking nonsense. Tell him to sit."

But the interpreter exercised his discretion, and merely told Mhau to be quick.

"There is not much more for me to say. I agree with the words spoken here by others, though some I do not properly understand. We thank you, *Nkosi,* for the books you have given us in which to write down marriages, but we do not want them to bring us into trouble. If, by not writing down every marriage, there is a case against us, we think it best if you take back the books. That is all, *Nkosi.*"

Mr. Tootles rose and again cleared his throat. "You have now had your say, and I have heard it. Now, remember what I told you and write every marriage in the books, and do not force your girls against their wishes. Government does not state that you must give up all your customs and become black Europeans, but asks you to trust us, since we know what is best. A thousand years ago our ancestors were at about the same level as you are now—they couldn't read or write and they had no machines. Well, it takes a long time to become civilized, but we are ready to help." He looked at his watch. "In short, you must stop all customs which are repugnant—" he hesitated, for he had forgotten the formula, then he continued bravely—"repugnant to morality and contrary to natural justice."

The interpreter said simply, "That are against the laws of the white men."

"Now you may go. I wish you to tell those who were not here what I have said."

It was twelve thirty-one. He had exactly fourteen minutes to write a note of the meeting for record purposes and get up to lunch. The policeman stood smartly at attention as he passed. The sun shone gaily and a gentle breeze stirred the flag.

The men remained behind to exchange news of kin and cattle, and to discuss the affairs of the country.

Mhau dismissed the meeting: "A thing of nothing."

"It is best at our homes," agreed Beta, hobbling by.

Mputuya was grimly unresponsive. Even his friend had not understood. Would these people never wake up?

The interpreter, now in the role of policeman, came to Mhau. "*Nkosi,* one of your men has a charge against him. His name is Mputuya Zwane. Where will I find him?"

"What is the charge?"

"Assault on a prophet."

"Haw. Bloody nonsense." (This in English.) "What are you going to do with my man?"

"Tell him to come to the *Nkosi* for the case."

Mputuya stepped forward. "I am Mputuya Zwane."

The policeman, impressed by his obvious size and strength, commented, "You could have killed the other." Then, recollecting his position, he said sternly, "The case will be spoken on Thursday of the coming week. You must be here early in the morning."

"O.K., Cop." Since he wasn't going to be arrested, he was a little ashamed of his initial panic and, by speaking English, tried to appear off-hand.

"Well, I was lucky to find you so quickly. I will tell the *Nkosi.*"

When he left, Mputuya spat. "That is what I meant when I said our present road is confused. Prophets and policemen."

Mhau calmed him. "No one will believe that humbug. You just see you are properly prepared. You have witnesses."

Mputuya felt so angry that he would gladly at that moment have bashed the prophet again—without provocation. Mhau found him poor company on the homeward journey and was glad when they arrived at the trading shop.

Simon had obviously been drinking steadily, but he remembered to ask the chief to send for the grain that his wives had found too heavy to carry, and Mhau, in anticipation of their welcome, genially promised to do so. A suggestion that Mputuya send his purchase the same way met with the curt refusal, "I have my strength."

"Of course." Mr. Simon hiccupped, unsteadily pouring Tears for the chief and for himself. "To the princess." He drained his tumbler.

"You drink too much, my white man," Mhau chided him, as though he were a wayward boy. "It doesn't help to drink so much alone. It is better to sit with many friends, and when the earth begins to move under you, to sing old songs. Then the words are there and you don't have to make up nonsense. To the princess!"

Simon giggled foolishly, then tried to explain. "We English often drink to the princess."

In the middle of Simon's rambling, Mputuya said with ill-concealed impatience, "*Nkosi Dlamini*. Time is leaving us."

"Indeed it is. Take our things. Stay well, Simon. Remember what I told you."

Mputuya put the torch batteries into his trouser pockets, shouldered his bag of seed, gripped his stick, and, with the minimum of farewells, led the way home.

"White men should not forget their laws, either," commented Mhau after a short silence. "Simon wriggles round like an earthworm. Perhaps he should marry a white woman. Though, of course," he conceded, "our women are more beautiful. Think of lying with a woman with hair like a horse's tail." And he rippled with mirth at the thought.

"That wife of Simon's hasn't any beauty," Mputuya remarked brutally. Then he added, "I wonder if Tootles would want you to register that marriage in your book."

As soon as the grain arrived the wives began to brew, though this meant extra heavy work in the busiest season of the year, when weeds sprang up after the first rains and choked the young plants; and even while the early plots were being cleared, late fields needed to be cultivated. But the "beer for the school dresses" was urgent, and Nabo Sicenga took over the preparation. She soaked the grain in water and spread it on the sun-warmed ground to sprout; she saw that enough fire-wood was collected for the boiling; when the grains had sprouted small white shoots, she called the co-wives and daughters to her yard to grind the malt into a thick, soft paste; and finally she supervised the pouring of the brew into two enormous pots over a crackling fire.

The smoke could be seen rising in thick clouds, so that people in neighbouring homesteads stopped and sniffed. "Ha, there will be beer at Mhau's in a few days' time." Nabo Sicenga and Nabo Totwa took it in turns to stand over the liquid as it frothed and boiled, and to scoop off the thick scum. The brew was taken into Nabo Sicenga's cooking hut and left to settle before being boiled a second time, and she poured a little through the long plaited strainer, squeezed out the husks, and sipped appreciatively from the gourd ladle, commenting, "Indeed, the taste is delicious."

For three days the brew bubbled gently in the hut, gaining strength, and its smell and taste grew steadily sweeter and more pungent till it reached the bloom of its maturity. Nabo Sicenga carried a big bowl to the chief, and kept another for the personal consumption of the wives; all the rest was for sale.

The writing of smoke had spread, and on the day of the sale, which had been carefully calculated for a Sunday, men and women from as far as Simon's shop and beyond poured into the chief's village. Some came with their own pots to carry the drink away to their homes, others drank with their cronies on the spot. They brought their shillings and sixpences, but some drifted in without money, hoping to be offered a sip to wet their parched throats; with Nabo Totwa as one of the hostesses, their hopes were never in vain, though Nabo Lamtana reminded her sharply that this was a sale, not a party.

Mputuya spent a shilling and sixpence, pleased in this way to contribute to the education of his friend's children. He felt in an expansive mood; he even called Mpisi to drink, for Mpisi never had any money of his own. Feka and Timba got more than their fill by wandering round cadging from different groups of drinkers. Feka had not spoken alone to Lamtana since the day that he had read the note brought by the policeman, but they had seen each other often and both had been aware of it. On this day, which was for her a day of triumph, she contrived to pass by him each time she carried a bowl for the mothers, and as he looked at her she turned away deliberately and provocatively. They could not speak otherwise in the crowd and with Mputuya so close.

"Come and drink up, friends," he called.

No one mentioned the case, though by now everyone knew that in a few days he would be brought before the commissioner. This was not the occasion to think of white man's laws.

Nabo Sicenga was famous for her beers—they were never too sour and never too mild, and they made the company happily intoxicated. One old woman tied round her ankles rattles of dried cocoons and began a sensuous, rhythmic dance, moving her hands slowly and gracefully and stamping down her feet. Nabo Totwa swung into a soft, seductive action, shaking her shoulders ever so slightly and keeping her smooth, round neck very still, and in her right hand she waved a small, stiff grass broom as daintily as any lady with a fan. Onlookers began to clap their hands and sing an old song.

> "*Li li li li.*
> Where is the mountain,
> *Li li li li.*
> Where is the mountain?"

She ended her dance on a shrill ululation, and a shudder of delight rippled from the tips of her fingers through her arms and shoulders and heavy skirt to her small-toed feet. Then she returned to her place and took her little son, whom Sicenga had been holding, in her arms and snuggled him to her.

By sunset all the beer had been drunk. Buyers and visitors left, most of them swaying happily and laughing more loudly than usual.

"I am drunk, beautifully drunk," yawned Nabo Totwa, sinking onto the floor of Nabo Sicenga's hut and stretching herself voluptuously. "Now I want my lord."

"How much money did we make?" asked Nabo Lamtana.

"I don't know and I don't care. My body is too happy for money."

"What do you ever care for except your body," said Nabo Lamtana viciously.

"Quietly, quietly, sisters," interposed Nabo Sicenga. "Go to your huts and sleep. Such sweet beer it was. This is not the time for quarrelling," and she helped Nabo Totwa firmly through the low doorway, and Nabo Lamtana swayed regally behind.

On getting back to her own sleeping hut, Nabo Sicenga carefully undid the thick waistband in which was tied the beer money. "It is heavy," she murmured with pleasure, "but I am too sleepy even to look at it." She took off her heavy skin apron and skirt, and tied the cloth round her waist again, just above a girdle of heavy red and white beads that she always wore and that shone against her skin. She unrolled her mat, pulled out her wooden pillow, and was just about to stretch herself out when she heard a familiar tread and Mhau himself came in. She sat up, immediately wide awake. "I did not think it was me you would rejoin tonight."

He replied softly, "Your beer is sweet. Let us go together."

She followed him to his hut.

Next morning all the wives collected to count the cash, which they poured into a heap on the floor. They sorted the different-sized coins into piles, and then laid them flat as they added each piece. Fifty-eight shillings and threepence. And of this, forty shillings belonged to Simon. Carefully they counted out and took away forty shillings.

"Only eighteen shillings." Nabo Totwa's lip quivered with disappointment. "Next time I will be more careful, and not give so much away for nothing."

Nabo Sicenga, who was in a wonderful mood, comforted her. "Don't worry. With this eighteen shillings we could make more beer. What a pity that I said Sicenga should have a dress as well. You know, my sisters, I don't believe that she really wants to go to school at all. She keeps on saying that the little ones will miss her. If Simon's wife hasn't yet made her dress, I'll tell her not to start and Simon could sell the material to someone else. It is such lovely material."

"Let the girls find out," said Nabo Lamtana, who had been pestered by her daughter to be allowed to go and see how the dresses were getting on. So, although two weeks had not yet passed, the mothers sent the three girls to investigate. It was the first time they had been permitted to go alone to the shop, and they felt very grown up.

Mr. Simon saw them come, and went out of his way to welcome them, but Lamtana shook him off politely. "We have come for our dresses, Simon. Forgive us. We have no time to chatter now. Later, perhaps." As they paraded off, he echoed Mpisi's opinion of her, "She is too proud," and sighed mournfully, "She is not my Lomusa."

The girls went straight to Mrs. Simon, who was greatly relieved to see them. She had discovered that the material was not as wide as she had thought, and the flowers introduced a further complication. She had therefore cut out only Lamtana's and Totwa's dresses and was awaiting further instructions. One yard was left over, and that was insufficient for the third dress. Would they, perhaps—this she advised—rather share the two dresses (though, of course, the fit would not be so good for Sicenga) and each go to school two out of three days, and use the material that was left over to make the necessary undergarments? She thought it might just be enough for that.

Sicenga hastened to inform Mrs. Simon that it was quite all right—she didn't really want so much to go to school, though she would have liked a dress. This evoked Lamtana's sense of justice. She did not want Sicenga to be deprived of a dress—had not Nabo Sicenga contributed as much as her own mother?—but she was not prepared to miss school on the days Sicenga was wearing her, Lamtana's, dress. She thought hard and was rewarded with an idea.

"Could we sell back the yard that is over and buy more of a cheaper material? If necessary, we could leave out bloomers and make a third dress."

"It would be different from yours and Totwa's," Sicenga protested.

"But you are the oldest, and it would be special," persuaded Lamtana.

Mrs. Simon was dubious, and suggested they ask Mr. Simon.

"First let us try on our dresses," begged Lamtana.

Warning them that she had chosen a style suitable for school, Mrs. Simon produced them. How beautiful. Look at all the hooks. The girls looked at them from all angles, and finally, with much giggling and extraordinary difficulty, wriggled into their first stitched clothing. Mrs. Simon showed them the cunning of the fastener.

"How these clothes love you," exclaimed Sicenga with unselfish admiration.

The skirts reached their knees, and all agreed that you could not know they were the only garment of modesty.

"Let's ask Simon to change the yard that's over, so that you can also have a dress to fit," urged Lamtana, a little breathless, having extricated herself from her uniform.

As the deputation entered the shop, Simon waved them to approach. "Time to talk now, eh?" he chuckled.

Lamtana put her proposition.

"Oh, no." He looked shocked. "I would never resell the left-over. It would be second-hand and no one would buy it. Follow Mrs. Simon's advice. Bloomers are a necessity for school." And he laughed encouragingly with all his teeth outward bound. Lamtana thought distastefully, "How ugly he is. Like a hippo," but she replied, "We will report your words to our mothers, White Man." Still, he gave her, and the others of course were included, a handful of sweets.

Back they went with Mr. Simon's refusal and Mrs. Simon's advice. The mothers reconsidered the position. Clearly Mrs. Simon had experience. Finally Nabo Sicenga ruled quite firmly that it would not be necessary for the three girls to share the two dresses; they had been cut to fit Lamtana and Totwa alone. "Sicenga"—and here she spoke for her daughter as well as herself—"will not mind. Perhaps she will go another year. Perhaps not."

"But how can we repay you?" asked Nabo Lamtana regally.

Nabo Sicenga said with a deep indolent smile, "It was nothing; we must help each other," but to herself she said, "It was worth it. If it is a girl, I will call her Velapi [From Whence Do You Come], and if a boy, Bongani [Let Us Praise]."

So, a few days later, Lamtana and Totwa each got a complete school outfit and Sicenga admired them without envy. Mrs. Simon had indeed kept her promise, and the dresses were different from any to be seen on any other school children, in Swaziland or out—and everyone agreed that they were more beautiful, and "fitted everywhere."

# 9 · THE PROPHET VERSUS MPUTUYA

Mputuya was at the court-house long before it opened. He left home when the morning star was still bright in the sky and he had not stopped once on the road or looked behind him.

To sustain him on his journey he had pushed down hunks of cold, stiff maize porridge, prepared by his wife the day before. Both she and Timba's mother were awake when he left, but the boys were still sleeping. He would have liked to have Feka with him for company, but tomorrow the holidays ended. He gave instructions to his wife for work to be completed that day, then said, "I am going. Stay well."

"Go well," the women chorused.

He walked quickly, and after he had passed Simon's shop he took from his pocket a scented root and chewed it vigorously. A few days ago he had consulted Hlubi, a squint-eyed *nyanga* who had built up a reputation for success in law cases, as well as in other disorders. Hlubi, for the small fee of two shillings and sixpence, "to open his medicine bag," had provided him with various ingredients with definite instructions.

"These must be stirred in water, and each morning wash with them. They will make you shine, and this"—he presented the root—"is to make your words sound good. It is Sweet Mouth; chew it on the road before you come to the court-house and before you speak. Leave before dawn, and do not rest on the way. Be there very early. That is very important with the white man. Do all I say and the ancestors will help you to succeed."

Mputuya did all that Hlubi said.

Lounging against the wall of the empty court-house near the steps, he waited. He could see the main road leading through the little outpost, past three general dealers' shack shops, past the post office and the bleak brick hotel. The remaining buildings of the township were partly hidden by tall wattle and eucalyptus trees that yielded a faint aromatic scent and heightened the feeling of sheltered emptiness. He began to feel thirsty. Beyond the hotel he knew of a homestead where there was always beer, and occasionally even brandy, for sale. One of the sons was chief waiter at the hotel and a friend of his. He started to walk towards this home, then, remembering Hlubi's instructions, turned around sharply and found himself almost face to face with the prophet, who had approached silently from the other side of the court-house. They glared at each other without speaking, each a little taken aback, and on guard. Mputuya thought, "His face is like a woman's except for that beard. He is weak, too, like a woman," and he held him in a full contemptuous stare. Just then a Swazi in what was once a white jacket came tearing along the road on a bicycle, obviously trying to be on duty for a time already past, but he braked dangerously to shout, "Hello, prisoners," before careening on again. He had broken the tension of the silence that bound the two protagonists; they separated, Mputuya back to his post at the steps, the prophet to the farthest corner of the yard.

The township was awakening. Mputuya watched a big dusty Buick with a Transvaal number plate drive past. The driver, a white man, sat alone in the front; at the back, also alone, sat his "boy." At the hotel the white man stopped and got out, and the black man also got out carrying his master's suitcase. Mputuya lost interest. Two Swazi sauntered down the street and greeted him politely, and they told each other from whence they came and asked his business at the court-house, to which he replied vaguely, "To speak about nothing much," and he asked them their business in the town and they replied equally vaguely, "Just come to buy." Time went slowly. The doors of the office were unlocked by a policeman. At eight A.M. sharp, Tootles arrived, walked past Mputuya, and disappeared into the office.

Near midday, Mputuya was awakened from a fine sleep in the sun by someone pushing him and guiding him to someone else, who shouted at him. The pusher was the illiterate policeman, and the shouter was the interpreter-policeman, who sat in a small room behind a desk with a few papers on the top and more in a basket on the floor.

"You are Mputuya Zwane."

"That is me."

"We have a complaint." And he read a long bit about assault to which Mputuya listened a little impatiently, waiting for his chance to speak, and at the end he was told to recount his version, which would also be recorded and taken to *Nkosi* Tootles for further investigation.

Mputuya began his story and the scribe laboriously took notes, interrupting the flow every few seconds with "Wait. I am still writing." When he wrote very wrong, he swore and threw the whole sheet into the basket under the desk and began again. Standing in front of the policeman in the small room Mputuya found it hard to be natural and talk with fluency, but the recorder finally took two full pages of "statement" to Mr. Tootles, saying sternly, "Stay there."

Staying there, Mputuya quickly took out his root and was still chewing it hard when the scribe returned and led him to Mr. Tootles.

Mr. Tootles lifted his innocent eyes and, seeing Mputuya towering over him from the door, thought, "That dangerous-looking brute." Having an excellent memory for faces—he once had declared that no two watches were ever identical—he recalled immediately his first meeting with Mputuya. But he gave no sign of recognition. He was not surprised to find that the charge against the fellow was one of assault. "However," he thought judicially, "I will not let myself be prejudiced," and he explained carefully through the interpreter that the charge was serious and that he hoped Mputuya had carefully considered the statement which he had made, since it could be used against him. He perused the scribe's report and anounced that Mputuya admitted inviting the prophet to his home to cure sickness and that while the prophet was laying hands on the patients, Mputuya struck him on the head with a stick. Was that true?

With Sweet-Mouth reasonableness, Mputuya tried to explain that that was true, but that something else was also true. The prophet was a fraud and when he laid his hands on the women, he did not heal them, but molested them. Mputuya could bring witnesses, his own wife and sister. (Tootles shook his head. "They are prejudiced.") And the children of the chief. ("Children?" he asked. Then again shook his head. "Minors are not trustworthy.") Others too. Tootles interrupted. "The witnesses can wait. Does he admit striking the man?"

"Yes, *Nkosi*."

"Good." He looked at his watch. How time flies. Nearly twelve forty-five already. "Come back at two o'clock sharp."

While Mputuya waited in the yard, Mr. Tootles went to lunch and returned as usual on the hour, having decided to forward the case to his superior (in the bureaucratic sense only) since his jurisdiction over serious crimes was limited (again bureaucratically). He had contemplated putting Mputuya under arrest, but rejected this for the very practical reasons that the main jail was at Mbabane, transport was a problem, and it was not easy to provide the necessary police escort. Through the interpreter he informed Mputuya that the case was not ended, and that he would arrange for him to appear in two weeks' time at the court of the "big chief" in Mbabane.

Mputuya swallowed loudly but showed no other sign of emotion, and getting into the yard, he spat out a great glob of root. At home he told his wife briefly what had happened and then went to report to the chief, who was disturbed that his daughters had been mentioned, until Mpisi said he agreed with Tootles that it was hard to believe the evidence of children, whereupon Mhau flared up. "Nonsense. They have better eyes than the old, and can tell truth as well as lies."

Mputuya's next visit was to Hlubi, the medicine man, who congratulated himself on having saved Mputuya from Tootles and gave additional medicine to work on the "big chief."

In the two weeks that followed, Mputuya toiled like one possessed, repairing the cattle byre, reshafting tools, drying underground granaries, ploughing and planting the fields, and trying to have everything in order in case he was sent to prison.

No bus left early enough for Mbabane, so he went on foot the day before he was to appear, sleeping at the homestead of old Helemu, a kinsman, on the way. There, too, it was agreed that the white man's law was simply wasting time, for he was absolutely innocent.

It was the rule for litigants at Mbabane to have their cases sifted by a man specially chosen for his character and knowledge of Swazi law, and only if he considered there was a case did he send it in to the commissioner. Fortunately for Mputuya, the holder of this key position, a Falstaff of a fellow named Potopoto, was not only one of his own regiment but of the same platoon and a good friend; when Mputuya entered the little out-room in which Potopoto conducted his investigation, he was warmly welcomed.

"*Hau*. So you have arrived, my age-mate. I heard you were coming. Sit down and tell me how the folk at home are keeping." They were in no hurry; there was much to tell each other and Mputuya listened with interest to Potopoto's news of his two sons who were schooling in the Union.

Eventually Potopoto said, "You had better tell me your story about the prophet. I have already heard his yarn." He listened appreciatively, his great bulk quivering with delight at Mputuya's "Amen, Amen," and at the conclusion, he wiped the tears from his merry little eyes and said, "Don't worry. I'll tell my white man what to say. I wouldn't even have reported the prophet's complaint to him if I didn't know that little chief Tootles had written him a long letter about it all." No, he didn't know what was in the letter, but he'd soon learn. Off he billowed on another gust of mirth, only to return a little later, obviously deflated.

"Let's go together," he said briefly. "Lizulu is waiting, and the prophet is with him."

Lizulu was as impressive as his name, which means The Sky —by which he was known to Swazi throughout the country. He was a man of vast expanse, with clear blue eyes set wide apart. His entire youth had been spent on a farm on the Swaziland border, and he was as familiar with the country and the customs of the people as his forefathers had been with the folk in his village in Derbyshire where for centuries his ancestors had been stonemasons. Towards the "raw Swazi," whom he described as "nature's gentlemen," he had a very deep affection; but towards the rest, especially those he labelled "mission boys," a definite distrust. "Civilized! Pah," he would say, "you mean degenerate." He also showed little tolerance for missionaries and traders, in general, and, let it be openly stated, most fellow administrators in particular. In his position as District Commissioner he felt constantly frustrated; he was outspoken in his

criticism both of "men in Whitehall" and of the recruits who
entered his service "stuffed with academic anthropology." He
was sufficiently well read and charming to have won as his wife,
in the face of considerable competition, a Devonshire schoolteacher of remarkable character who had come to the country
on a visit. In the official bureaucracy his main defect, which
increased with the years and the postponement of promotion,
was his independence. And it was this very quality that the
Swazi respected in him.

Tootles' report, which Lizulu was holding when Mputuya was
brought in, contained a postscript: "P.S. The defendant seems a
bit crazy. [signed] A. Tootles."

Lizulu looked sharply at Mputuya.

"Stand there," he commanded, not bothering to use an interpreter. The prophet was out of Mputuya's reach. "Let us sift
this case." Briefly he outlined the charge as recorded, and asked
the prophet if it was correct.

"Yes, *Nkosi,* exactly; he wants to kill me."

Lizulu noticed, with sudden sympathy, Mputuya's glare of
contempt, which said plainly, "If I want to kill you, you can't
stop me."

Lizulu then read the statement accredited to Mputuya and
asked if it was correct.

"No, *Nkosi.* That which is written down is not all. Indeed, it
is so little of the truth that it makes lies."

"Speak, then. Tell me what happened that afternoon."

"*Nkosi,* let me start from the beginning."

"I am listening."

Mputuya found it easy to talk in front of Lizulu, whose eyes
met his without hostility and who listened without interruption.
At the description of the prophet's antics, Lizulu felt his gorge
rise in sympathy. "Elmer Gantry," he muttered to himself. "The
old hypocrite."

When Mputuya had done, he asked, "Before you struck him,
did you tell him to stop?"

"Yes. I shouted with all the sound I could. But his ears were full of Satan."

Lizulu smiled. Mputuya did not smile back.

"I see you are not a convert."

"No, Lizulu. I offer to the ancestors."

"Good." He turned to Potopoto. "You said you knew this man?"

"Very well. He is a good man. He knows he is too strong, so he does not like to fight others."

"That scar on your cheek. Was that from a fight?"

"No, *Nkosi*. I was hit by a stone in the mine."

"I see." He, too, hated mines.

He looked hard at Mputuya and saw in the scarred face no craziness, only the sadness of an unarmed warrior. He turned to the prophet. "He hit you for a reason. Do not again lay your hands on other men's wives, blaming it on a Holy Spirit. Someone might really kill you next time. Go, both of you, and don't trouble me again."

Mputuya felt as though his chest would burst open, and he could find no words. *"Nkosi,"* Potopoto prompted him gratefully.

*"Nkosi,"* Mputuya repeated.

Lizulu had dismissed them. He gave a final glance at Tootles' report and at the bottom, under the postscript, wrote in his big writing, "Not as crazy as A. Tootles," and initialled it T.D.B. He put the report into a file, labelled it Prophet vs. Mputuya Zwane, No Case, and stacked it neatly on his shelf. Then he settled down with relish to write a "Brief Memorandum on the Necessity of Increasing the Power of Traditional Native Authorities with Regard to the Present System of Recruitment of Administrative Personnel." He worked happily till long after dark, and then walked home to his wife.

Mputuya had left some time before.

When he had walked out of the office into the sun, his body had felt so light and weak he could hardly support it. He scarcely noticed the prophet slip past, out of his life and out of the lives of those he loved.

He waited until late afternoon for Potopoto to finish his work and then went with him to his home beyond the township boundary. He sent one of Potopoto's sons for a shillingsworth of beer, and they drank deeply and talked and sang, but it was not the beer that made him dash with huge dancing leaps along the road towards home, brandishing his stick and composing a song which later became famous:

> "I have seen one white man
> Who is a person.
> *Dji oh dji oh.*
> I have seen Lizulu,
> Bright as the sun.
> *Dji oh dji oh.*"

He slept again at the home of Helemu, his kinsman, who would not let him leave till late the following morning, and regaled him with the best of fare. It was past noon by the time he arrived at the chief's village, and the glad news had raced ahead of him. In the stuffy classroom Totwa whispered to Lamtana, "Feka's father is saved."

"I knew already," was the prompt reply.

She never got over the exquisite thrill of writing her name—. Lamtana Nkosi Dlamini. She wrote it over every spare inch of her slate, and when sitting on the ground at home she would trace with her finger each letter, delicately, lovingly, in the sand. Then, with the palm of her hand, she would carefully cover it over as though hiding something sacred, a deep core of self. She learned to write her name before she could read or write anything else, and while Totwa was still struggling with AH, BU.

At first she was wildly enthusiastic; even when it rained, and the children nearest the school stayed at home, she would wait for the first lull—and then only not to wet her dress too much —and run as fast as her long, firm legs could move through the mud, hoping not to be too late. She would have liked to be the first to come and the last to leave, but Totwa, who from the beginning had said gaily that "learning is too quiet," was prepared to come last and leave first. Teacher and pupils judged time by the sun, and when Miss Sibanze was ready and thought a sufficient number of pupils had arrived, she would tell one of the bigger boys to "hit the iron," which job was happily performed by vigorously striking together two pieces of rusty metal. The pupils trooped in, and stood still till Miss Sibanze said piously, "Good morning, children."

"Good morning, Teacher."

"Let us sing and praise the Lord." She chose a hymn from a well-thumbed little black book, and they sang in Zulu loudly and happily till she decided they had praised the Lord sufficiently and should settle down to more mundane activities.

"Sit."

Since there were only a few benches, the highest grade had the privilege of both discomfort and elevation and the two other grades occupied the remaining floor space.

Of the fifty-six students in her register, not more than forty-five were usually present on any single day; if the weather was sufficiently fine, one of the classes would be sent outside, enabling Miss Sibanze to walk round the room and supervise.

Miss Sibanze had entered Lamtana and Totwa, who were in the lowest—and largest—class, as swelve years of age. Nabo Lamtana remembered that both children were born in the year the Locust Regiment was mobilized by the Swazi king. Miss Sibanze, not quite sure of the date, rubbed her nose thoughtfully and said, "Nineteen thirty-three," and from this she calculated aloud, marking off each year on a finger, 1933, 1934, 1935, until she came to 1951. "You are eighteen," she said triumphantly. Then she gave them a sharp over-all look. "But you are younger. You are fourteen."

The girls were impressed by Miss Sibanze's ability, and a little terrified by her techniques of instruction. If the children made too many mistakes, or spoke to each other in class, she would call in a droning voice that Totwa copied best by pushing out her lower lip and pinching her nostrils tight together, "Come here, you. Show me your hands." Her switch was a branch of tough evergreen shrub, and the victims agreed with grudging admiration that "she hits well." After her first experience of Miss Sibanze's discipline, Totwa complained that she could not write with such sore hands, and spent a few happy days weeding the gardens with Sicenga.

"I don't like a stranger, even a teacher, hitting my child," her mother stated indignantly.

"It is nothing," philosophized Nabo Lamtana. "We grew up with beatings; they strengthen the young."

"Well, let her strengthen your young," said Nabo Totwa hopefully, but fearing that this would never be. Lamtana was much too smart.

It was soon clear that Totwa was not cut out for study. "I get terribly hungry and sleepy, just sitting," she confided to Sicenga. "You're much better off not thinking so hard, Sister. Next term I will help with the little ones and the fields, and let Lamtana go on her own; I don't think anyone will mind. I'll give her my school clothes, they'll still be new."

Lamtana did not complain, and fought against the sleepiness that made it hard for her on the summer days to look at her slate without seeing the letters blur and dance. A new world was opening for her, a world of which she had received a few vivid glimpses. A young schoolboy reading a letter to a group of illiterate elders, including her own father; a woman cutting dresses by pattern and sewing on a machine; things beyond imagination pictured in a pile of books and magazines. She wanted to know more. She began to visit the Simons' house frequently, accompanied by a sister or a nurse-girl to one of the younger children to give respectability to her visits; she knew well that she would be stopped and probably beaten if she went alone.

Both Simons found it pleasant to while away an hour or so

with a listener so eager to hear about "styles" and "city life" and "the world" at large. "If you want to know things," Simon said with a wink, "come to Simon," and in his eagerness to please he bared his long yellow canines in an amiable grimace.

The Simons' establishment was novel and exciting. Their bedroom in particular intrigued her—the vast double bed (how could you sleep so high and not fall off?), the soft white pillow with the words "Jesus Loves Me" embroidered in pink-and-green chain stitch and French knots, the big round mirror (in which she could watch herself for hours), the wash stand with a green marble top, the white china jug painted with pink flowers, the flowered rug on the floor, in fact, the whole incredible range of possessions that set this home apart from all others she knew. It was strange to think that Mrs. Simon was a Swazi like herself.

Not only things, but a treasure of ideas opened through the new magic of learning. The seamstress-housekeeper became transformed into "The Lady of the Lamp" as she told Lamtana about Florence Nightingale, who gave light and strength to the wounded and dying. Fancy! Mrs. Simon herself had done a year of nursing in a mission hospital in Zululand. Pity she never would say why she had stopped this noble work, or how she came to marry Simon. She never spoke ill of anyone, and yet had much to talk about, once she had lost her shyness. Her great hero was St. George. To him, Lamtana gave Feka's handsome face.

Occasionally, Simon regaled the women with tales of places that he claimed to have visited. He had a book full of pictures of ships. But he never mentioned any person except himself, the strident character of his own travelogue.

"He talks as though he had travelled the whole world," Lamtana confided to Totwa, "but I don't believe him, because if he had, why would he choose to stay here?"

"This is the most beautiful place in the world," Totwa answered, "and I suppose he is glad to have been lucky enough to find it."

"No. It is he who told me there are more beautiful countries, and if he has been there, he should know."

"Perhaps it's the women here."

Lamtana looked at her. Was she hinting? But Totwa's black eyes were without guile. "Perhaps. He doesn't speak of his women."

She began to lose some of her enthusiasm for the drab, stuffy classroom and sandy playing field. She began to master the mystery of letters and as her skill in reading improved, her interest in what Miss Sibanze could offer waned. The schoolbooks were dull compared with women's illustrated magazines. They were written in stiff, uncolloquial English by a white "expert" in Bantu languages. The characters in her reading book were animals or cannibals, and the stories about them bore little resemblance to the long tales that she had heard and relished from infancy.

She might have slacked in her school attendance had it not been for Feka. Though they sat in different parts of the room—he being in the highest class—they managed to communicate, and she would listen to his replies to Miss Sibanze's questions, admiring his cleverness. Next year, if he passed, Miss Sibanze could teach him no more.

"Why have you gone to school so long?" Totwa asked him.

"Father said I must learn," was the simple, direct reply.

"I see." She, too, accepted that there was no question of disobeying Mputuya. "I pity you, though," she continued thoughtfully. "I won't study much longer. It is too disappointing." Then she flashed him a quick smile and a knowing look at Lamtana. "But there is another teacher for you."

Lamtana tossed her head; the mop of tight, long ringlets that even Miss Sibanze's disapproval had not made her crop in "believer style" danced across her face. "You'll be a fool," she said disdainfully, and was rewarded by Feka's laugh.

Nearly every day after school Feka and a couple of pals would be waiting for the girls a little distance along the road.

"*Hau!*" Lamtana would exclaim in surprise. "Where did you come from?"

"It is wonderful"—he would beam—"how often we meet on the road."

Soon all the pupils had noticed where Feka's heart was leading him. Once he gave Lamtana a large cake of Velvet Skin Soap, and another time a red comb. But all this had to be hidden from the elders, for she was still a *litshitshi,* newly matured with virgin pointed breasts, and her father was the chief.

Sometimes the school children would pair off and lie and play together, exploring never-ending wonders by techniques defined by ancient custom. After a while Lamtana went with Feka, but when Feka, bursting with rude young virility, tried to reach beyond that which custom permitted the unmarried, Lamtana checked him crudely. And once Lamtana, abandoning herself to the ecstasy of exploration, urged him further. Then it was Feka who suddenly grew afraid and withdrew with surly embarrassment. After the initial shock, Lamtana thought with a sudden rush of mature tenderness, "He's just a child."

Sometimes Timba in his ragged clothes managed to join the school children, and with a roguish smile would ask them to teach him the things they had learnt. If Totwa was there to play Miss Sibanze, they would give him a mock lesson, and laugh together at his mistakes. He learned quickly and forgot blithely; he preferred hunting field-mice, trapping birds, playing games of skill, and making loud declarations of love to all the young girls. But he was a little shy of Lamtana, perhaps also a little jealous. He loved Feka very deeply, and could read his face better than most people could read a book. "Do not go too far," he warned him. "Remember, she's still young and the child of the chief."

One day Miss Sibanze, while supervising a class in the yard, saw a fluttering piece of blue writing paper and, having taken the trouble to pick it up and read it, returned to the classroom. She was the only person to wear shoes, and these made a padding noise that always warned the children of her approach. There was a quicker beat to her walk than usual, and when she shouted, "Children," something extra in her nasal voice, a dangerous sugary note, startled them upright.

"Who wrote this?" No sound. Her tiny flat nose twitched with pleasure. She stroked it. Again she weighed her question. The silence stiffened. "I will read it to you." She simpered. " 'Princess. Greetings. How is your health? My health is bad. I do not sleep because of you. Your beauty wakes me. Please I beg reply. I who am yours.' " Titters from some. Again silence.

"Feka,"—the voice rose high—"this is your writing. Come here." The slow shuffle of feet. "Quickly." Reluctantly he moved nearer. "Show me your hands." The stick sang down with vicious relish; a few children winced. Lamtana felt each blow—and was glad. One. Two. Three. Four. Five. Up to twelve. Feka made no sound. "Go back to your place. Let this never happen again. Get on with your work."

As soon as school was over, Lamtana rushed home, unwilling to see or speak to anyone. She felt guilty and humiliated, and more angry than sympathetic. Nearly every boy had a sweetheart to whom he sent notes, surreptitious and always unsigned; but never before had anyone been so careless as to let evidence of an attachment fall into Miss Sibanze's clutches.

For several days Lamtana deliberately avoided looking at Feka or meeting him. In vain he sent messages through Totwa, using Timba as his spokesman, since Totwa's loyalty to Lamtana made her refuse to speak directly to the offender.

"Beautiful one," Timba would begin engagingly, "tell your sister to look at my brother. He will die unless she forgives him. Does she want that? He can't understand how the letter blew out of his pocket, into that Bushman's hands. Go along, Totwa, help him. Besides, he is bothering me too much." Totwa listened, trying to appear indifferent, chewing a stalk of grass, stroking her smooth arms, and then replied, "I've already spoken to her, and she closes her ears. What you said to me today is what you said to me yesterday, and the other days, and that didn't change her heart. Poor Feka, I pity him. But what can I do? It is the male and female fire-stick." This business over, they chatted of other things and laughed together. For who could help laughing with Totwa?

It is impossible to tell how much longer the impasse might have lasted had not Feka himself stopped Lamtana before school one morning. She was alone and as she was about to walk past him, he grabbed her arm and said in a voice trembling with excitement, *"Mntan'enkosi.* Look at me. Hear me." She tried to push past, but he held her arm. "Listen to me. You must. I'm going away."

She stood still. He stuttered, "Yes, I'm leaving here. I had to tell you. I'm going away." The words fell over each other in their urgency.

"It is true. Father wants to send me to school in the Colony. I will stay there night and day." He paused and looked at her standing very straight and motionless. "So I think I am going, Lamtana," he ended a little lamely.

*"Hau."* Her voice was small. "Are you leaving us?"

"As I said, Lamtana, Father is arranging it."

"When are you going?"

"Next term, when I pass."

"Why is he sending you so far?"

"He has chosen the school to which the nation sent our king." He hesitated. "Father saw my hands." Then, at the look of dismay, hurried on. "He does not know why she hit me." He grinned. "I lied fine. He was pleased she hit so hard but said I needed men to teach me."

"Are you glad to be going?"

Very slowly, face half turned from her, he replied, "No, I don't want to leave you." He moved his head slowly to look at her straight.

The clang of iron pushed their eyes apart. Feka went first. Lamtana arrived later.

He was waiting alone for her on the road after school, and this time she did not avoid him. They went together through the grass to their place near the river, a quiet, hidden place that he had discovered, where the drooping boughs of a tree made a small shelter and the sun shone through in tiny chinks of light. They sat a little distance from each other and talked for a while of school and home; then she said, to flatter him, "You were a man indeed when Miss Sibanze struck you."

"I could have hit her harder," he boasted.

She said casually, "You will find smart girls in the Colony."

"They will be Xhosas without proper manners."

"You will get used to them."

"No." She was closer to him now and her dress revealed her shapeliness.

He leaned over and pressed her breast.

"Let me do it first with you, and I will not touch them." He scarcely recognized his own voice.

She drew back.

"Come on," he pleaded, and caressed her again.

She arose. He saw her thighs, dazzling and promising, and tried to grasp them. She stumbled and he caught her. "Let me." He stroked her clumsily, harshly.

"Help me, Lamtana, help me."

"No," she shouted, pushing him from her. "Do you want to leave me with a baby just because you're going away? You can run to Goli, but I can't. You men are all *Tsotsis,* thinking only of your own pleasures. Have you no decency?"

"I don't like leaving you for others," he mumbled. "Everyone will want you when I am gone. How can they deny themselves your beauty, how can you refuse when the red blood sings? Oh, my girl," he appealed, "I am afraid others will not show my restraint."

"Your restraint," she mocked. "My strength was your restraint. If I can push you off, I can push off others."

And that was all the comfort and reassurance she would give him then.

In the classroom next morning she felt his eyes constantly upon her, and Totwa whispered with genuine concern, "Why are you shaking? Are you sick?"

"Perhaps I have a little fever."

"Then I'll ask Teacher if I can take you home" was the prompt, not entirely disinterested response.

Miss Sibanze gave her frigid consent and the girls left quickly.

On the way Totwa asked, "You're crying?"

An indrawn sob was the reply.

"Where is your pain? Tell me."

"Everywhere, my whole body burns."

"Are you crying from the pain?"

Lamtana could resist no more. She wailed, "Feka is going. Going to Goli."

"Is that it! You knew that yesterday, so why are you crying today?"

As the sobs continued, Totwa tried to comfort her. "You'll miss him, but he'll come back. Anyway, he hasn't even left yet! You are a stupid. But I'm glad I took you home. I'm really tired of school."

Miss Sibanze grew so agitated as the examination day drew near that even Lamtana suffered the stick. This so infuriated her mother that she sent for the teacher to come and see her, impervious to the sarcasm behind Nabo Totwa's remark, "You should be glad to have your child strengthened."

"She could never strengthen my child, that Bushman," exploded Nabo Lamtana, insulting the teacher with the most degrading appellation she could conceive, and following this with a stream of obscenities engulfing Miss Sibanze, her father, her mother, and all her kin and associates.

Miss Sibanze, formally attired with scarf as well as beret, stood up for herself with considerable—and unexpected—force. "A teacher," she pointed out rudely, "is not like a husband; she does not choose favourites." While she agreed that Lamtana was very smart, she did not know everything, and could not come to school to dream; on the fatal day Miss Sibanze had had to shout her name three times before she even heard.

"Shout louder," snapped the irate mother, "but do not strike. I am the one to do that, if necessary."

"My position is important. The inspector from Mbabane wants good results."

"Don't do it again," threatened the mother, "or you won't have a smart pupil like Lamtana to show off to your inspector."

He arrived by car soon after school was assembled, a big man with a shock of white hair, a lined, tired face, and an enormous hooked nose. The children jumped like soldiers to their feet, and he clumped in his heavy shoes to the chair, flapped his hand downward in a weary gesture, and said in Zulu, "Good morning, children. Sit." Then, realizing the crush that would be created, quickly thought again and said, "No. Stand." Then he told Miss Sibanze, who was twitching at his side, that he would examine one class at a time. "Send the others out to play and we'll begin with the first grade."

He watched the children, of all sizes and ages in a motley assortment of "uniforms," troop out, and then turned to look at the pupils remaining in the room. What bright shining faces, smooth and open and expectant. He smiled. They smiled back. Miss Sibanze frowned. The smiles froze.

He spoke to her in English. "Let us start with reading."

She answered in her most correct grammar, "That is right, sir."

She instructed the class to get out their reading books, three and sometimes four children to one book.

"Would anyone like to begin?" he asked, and since there was no reply he said genially, "Well, Teacher, whom shall it be?"

"Lamtana, sir. She reads excellently well."

Lamtana read a few sentences about a cunning weasel, and he listened. "Good. Now let's hear the girl next to her."

"Please sir, she does not read so excellently well."

"Let her try."

Totwa struggled. He stopped her. "Next." He got the level.

"Now for sums. Tell them to put up their hands if they know the answers." On the board he wrote 3 + 3.

Fingers wriggled rapidly. Hands shot up. "Yes. You."

"Sikis," came the happy answer in English.

"Good. Now this one. Five plus three. Try not to count on your fingers." A pause. He looked down. Toes wriggled. A hand shot up. He nodded.

"Naiyin."

"No. Eight," shouted Lamtana, unasked.

"Very good."

Between fingers and toes the class had acquitted itself well enough at addition.

"Now take away six from nine?" It was like watching a scale played on keys and pedals. One hand shot up.

"Yes, Lamtana?"

"Tree, sir."

"Right. Now ten take away four."

Again the same hand. He waited. Her other hand shot up. He chuckled. "Well?"

"Sikis, sir."

"Right again." He turned to Miss Sibanze. "Your star pupil, I see."

Miss Sibanze beamed. "She is the child of Chief Mhau."

"Oh. So he's sending his children to school now. That's an advance." He looked again at Lamtana, noting the oval face, the long sweeping lashes over the eager wide-set eyes, the nose flat without being fleshy, the wide forehead, the generous mouth. Yes, beauty and intelligence were there; if only Miss Sibanze knew how to teach. He proceeded with the examination. It was a long journey, and he wanted to be back for lunch. By the time the third class came in he was already rather hungry and decidedly thirsty, but he was too much of a gentleman to imbibe in the presence of Miss Sibanze from the little flask he carried with him. (And, of course, he could never share that with her.)

The senior pupils were often the most disappointing, their early enthusiasm (if it had existed) having been effectively stifled. He shortened his technique.

He paged through Book III. "Tell the best pupil to read page fourteen, 'The Cannibals Are Coming!' "

"Tina. Read page fourteen."

Tina stood up. A tall, thin girl with widely spaced teeth that seemed to be on guard in a broad expanse of mouth. Each word thudded out, loud and clear.

"Good. Now tell your worst pupil to continue."

Miss Sibanze thought quickly. She refused to show how bad that was!

"Feka," she said, "continue."

The inspector was somewhat surprised to hear the lad read almost as well as the girl. He was, of course, much bigger than most of the others in the class. Very well grown, though. Nothing stupid to look at. Remarkably handsome, in fact. Almost a man. It would be better for him to be working instead of loafing with youngsters in the schoolroom. There should be a regulation against this indiscriminate mixing of the ages. Often led to trouble. He looked Feka sternly in the eye. "What are you going to do when you leave school at the end of this year, if you pass?"

"He is going to high school, sir," Miss Sibanze bobbed eagerly. "His father wants him to be a teacher."

"A teacher. But isn't he the worst in the class? What is his mark?" She felt him look at her so suspiciously that all she exposed was the top of the newly acquired green beret. He glanced down at the register. It told him as much. Feka's marks were as high as Tina's.

Well, well. This Miss was not such a fool after all! He picked a name himself. One really low. The owner of the name and marks read. The inspector was satisfied; Miss Sibanze burned.

"Now for arithmetic." They were about to start when from the teacher came a high feminine squeak, and her head, which had remained bent since the discovery of the little deception, jutted rigidly from her neck in hypnotized horror. The children craned forward. On the floor was a toad, its bloated sides puffing like bellows, its bulging eyes rolling. It had materialized from nowhere.

"What's the matter?" asked the inspector. He leaned over the desk. "Oh, a frog. Throw it out the door."

Not a person moved.

"Throw it out, I said. Have you never seen a frog before? Surely you aren't afraid of it, Teacher?" Exasperated now, he shouted, "Well, if you're too much of a lady to touch it, get one of the boys to throw it out." His eyes lit on Feka. "Here, lad, throw it out."

From under the beret came an imploring voice. "Feka, throw it out."

Very slowly, as though held back by the soles of his bare feet, Feka approached. The toad hopped sideways, a dirt-streaked bubble. The children nearest screamed with fear. The hideous creature lay palpitating in Feka's reach. With a sudden pounce he had it in his hand. A thick white milk oozed onto his fingers. He walked to the door and flung the thing out with all his strength, and there was a sick, explosive plop. He looked with disgust at his hands, wiped them helplessly on his trousers, and walked back to his place.

Sensing more to the incident, but knowing from experience the uselessness of direct questioning, the inspector said quietly, "Well done, boy. Now let's get on with the work."

Things went badly after that. Even when the children knew the answers, they said them stupidly, and Miss Sibanze was obviously distraught. She began picking her nose and then poking her finger under the beret and scratching gently at her scalp. After a short while the inspector told her to dismiss the class.

He leaned back, exhausted mentally and physically. Looking round the now empty room, he spoke half to her and half to himself. "How can I expect better results? For twenty-five years I've battled for better conditions—more schools, qualified teachers, and equipment, and always the old answer, 'No money.' It's more than that. Damn it. It's no desire really to get things changed. We're afraid to give up our pretence of superiority. School after school with fresh, impressionable material turned out shapeless, misinformed. In this school now, that girl Lamtana." It reminded him of where he was and he turned to Miss Sibanze, who was standing with a bewildered, pained expression on her plain face and a short finger with blunt nail rubbing up and down her nose in her effort to concentrate, she was not sure on what.

"Tell me, Teacher, why did the frog upset you all?"

To this she responded so eagerly as to forget her grammar, "Sir, it's a good classes, but everybody know that toad show witchcraft. I not think who put it there."

"No. No. No one put it there. Surely it could come of its own accord through the open door after yesterday's storm. It was probably sitting in a corner, finally got bored—understandably —and wanted to move out. That's not witchcraft."

This matter-of-fact explanation made her again acutely self-conscious. "Yes. Sir. Truly, sir."

After a pause, he asked her how she liked her post, to which she replied that she was "sitting it quite nice."

"Let me see. As far as I remember, you have passed Standard Five."

"Yes, sir," adding with modest pride, "I failed Standard Six."

He told her that he thought she should perhaps try to teach the children more concretely—use bits of wood or stones for arithmetic—pay more attention to handwork and gardening. He gave her a few words of encouragement and said he must be going, adding as an afterthought that she had better pass the lot. This seemed a happier solution than failing the lot; apart from a couple of the brightest there was really little to choose between them, and they all needed hope. Damn it.

She accompanied him respectfully to his car. The pupils were gathered round, commenting on its parts and make, but he noticed that Feka and Lamtana were a little apart, joking together. Damn again. He had a sensitivity to this sort of thing.

As he approached, all talking stopped, only the eyes watched and questioned. He said good-bye courteously to the teacher but offered no handshake. He gave a sort of salute to the children as he drove off.

Miss Sibanze summoned them back to the classroom. Relieved that the visit was over, she was still badly put out by the ordeal and began to scold them all in a cracked voice, while they listened tolerantly. She was without her stick that day.

Lamtana, well aware of the impression she had made, was elated by her own brilliance, and decided to continue with school the following year. It did not worry her that Totwa, who had decided that she had learned enough, would not return, but would stay with Sicenga and the others. Nabo Totwa and Nabo Sicenga had long ago agreed that a girl's place was at home. Lamtana's mother, however, was pleased with her daughter's choice and proud of her progress (Totwa told everyone that Lamtana was the brightest girl in the school), nor did the expense trouble her as it did the others. When she heard how well Lamtana had done in the examination, she praised her with a shilling piece, and sold a goat to Simon for material for a new dress.

With the shilling Lamtana bought herself a note-book and pencil. On the cover she wrote her name and on the first page put a title, "Thots of Lamtana Nkosi Dlamini." Her writing and spelling in English were atrocious, but she seldom halted for a word. "My life now is gud. It is hapy. Utha peepl have only too ies to help them see, but I have for. Too ies with which I was born and too which I have fownd threw lurning. No I have many ies, as many as there are stars, becoz I can reed of as many stranj things and plases. My new ies are briter than the ies in my own hed, and what the ies see, the hart enjows. With my for ies I see my friend."

She told Feka about her book of "thots," and he was surprised. How did she come to think of such things?

"I am smart," she stated simply.

"Will you show me?"

"Never. Those that I want you to know, I will write in my letter to you." Tears filled her eyes at this self-inflicted reminder of his impending departure, and he comforted her, but during his few remaining weeks at home they hardly ever managed to be alone together.

Mputuya reckoned it was time to make the final arrange-
ments for Feka's further education, but before settling on the
king's old school, he thought he would discuss the matter with
someone of experience. And who more suitable than his old
friend Potopoto, of the court-house, who, he remembered, had
two sons both "schooling" somewhere in the Republic. If they
were at the famous school in the Cape, his choice was easy,
otherwise, though it was doubtful if there could be any better,
there was much to be said for Feka's being together with sons
of his friend. Not only would they alleviate the initial loneliness
that Mputuya knew would inevitably afflict his son, but they
would possibly check any irresponsible inclinations stirred by a
new independence.

So Mputuya, accompanied this time by Feka, walked again

all the way to Mbabane. Feka would have liked to ask his father many questions about his plans, but accepted that he did not have the right to do so, and politely walked ahead in almost complete silence. When they met others on the road, Mputuya did not mention his mission, afraid that his ambition for his son might wake the malice of the envious; if asked by the curious where they were going, he said with simple pride, "We have affairs in Mbabane."

They went straight to Potopoto's office, and Potopoto welcomed them warmly. "You didn't kill a prophet this time, did you?" he said, laughing so heartily that tears oozed from his eyes and his chin heaved. He gladly left off the work on which he was engaged to converse with his friend. When they came around to the real purpose of the visit, Potopoto suggested that Mputuya and Feka go home with him that afternoon and speak to his sons, who were home for their holidays. He himself was well satisfied with their school, St. Cuthbert's in Johannesburg. They were both doing well; the elder, in Junior Certificate, next year would study to be a teacher, and the other, who was about the same age as Feka, was already in Standard Five. Though they had learned much, they had not lost respect and always brought back reports of good conduct from the Father. It is true that the fees were high, and the boys complained about the food, but they looked fit enough and they had no sores. Of course, as Mputuya knew, and here Potopoto leaned over to his friend and gave him a solid, friendly punch on the chest, they were not as strong as their own generation, and the boys' teeth were like the soft bread they ate, not like ivory or hard grains of corn. But that was the modern boy, not the school.

Mputuya and Feka wandered through Mbabane till Potopoto was ready to take them to his home, and Feka, who had never been to the town before, was much impressed by so many shops in one street, by the smartly dressed men and girls, and by the roaring traffic. He could not believe it when his father said, "This is nothing to Goli," but he did not express his disbelief.

At Potopoto's the two sons entertained the guests, and Mputuya, looking at and listening to them, could not but compare them with his own son, who, though perhaps less learned in books, was undoubtedly more handsome and quite as well mannered. Still, they seemed good enough lads, nicely spoken, not cheeky, and willing to help. So it was all settled. They slept at Potopoto's that night, and the next morning Potopoto got his older boy to write to the Father in charge of St. Cuthbert's, Johannesburg.

On the way back they stopped at the home of old Helemu. Feka was particularly respectful towards this relation, who expected to be told all important affairs of the family, and who was always full of advice. Helemu was delighted to see his kinsman, and soon they were reminiscing about their last very happy meeting when Mputuya had composed his now famous song about Lizulu, and they sang it together again with gusto. Helemu then gave Feka such a long lecture on how to comport himself in the city, particularly on what not to do, that the boy was glad to leave early the following morning.

His head was full of the prospects of Goli, and when he met Lamtana after his return, he began telling her all about the wonders of the city, glowing with such happiness that she could only nod and utter little *Hau*'s of surprise. He talked and laughed much and did not notice how unusually quiet she was.

For the next few weeks he was kept very busy by his father, who, because of the heavy expenditure the school would involve, had decided to stay at home for the shortest possible period and leave together with his son. Yet Feka managed to slip away occasionally when his day's work was done, and Lamtana, eager to see him, would usually be waiting for him at the river-bank. One afternoon he persuaded her to come back with him to his home to see the things they had bought from Simon's for the new school, and she went with him to his hut but avoided the women of his home. With great pride he displayed a black blazer and long trousers and a new khaki shirt, all neatly folded in a wooden trunk pasted over with many-coloured papers and bought specially for him. It seemed to them that they had been there only a few minutes when they heard Timba returning with the cattle from the pastures. Lamtana jumped up, fearful of her sisters, and, ignoring Timba's sallies, rushed home. It was one thing meeting in secret at the river, and another going to the home of the boy in public.

For a few days before he was to leave, Feka was a king. Relatives—even old Helemu—travelled to see him, and friends came to say good-bye, bringing him small gifts and big advice. Mputuya and his wife were proud and hospitable, and Feka noticed how much tasty food his mother cooked for him. She had borne five children, three boys and two girls, and he was the only one who had survived. It was on the death of her youngest, a baby not yet weaned, that she had become a Zionist Christian, and morning and evening she prayed, "God help my child grow into manhood." Mputuya had never interfered with her new faith. "It happened through trouble," he explained. "Women have not the fortitude of men. Women need children, as men need women." Yet he himself had never taken more than one wife, and though many people, including his friend the chief, had criticized him and even tried to entice him into a second marriage, he always had the excuse that he was too often away from home and the women would quarrel in his absence. A few of his friends blamed his wife, saying she should have taken the initiative, but no one ever had the impudence to say this in her presence. And there was no doubt that most people feared and respected this gaunt, strong woman, so devoted to her husband and her son, and considerate towards her ailing sister-in-law.

The day before the departure, Mputuya went at dawn to the cattle byre and, standing next to his finest ox, a white beauty with a streak of red-brown down the right side and fascinatingly twisted horns, he spoke to the dead, rededicating to them the best of his beasts, in return for protection for his family in his

absence and for his son and himself on their journey. With eyes
to the east he spoke to them: "I am going away again, my
fathers. Do not forget this home. I do not forget you. Let my
child that is returning with me stay in health and knowledge.
And let the orphans who remain behind find food. Listen, you
are the strong and wise men whose voices roared wisdom in the
council." And as he sang the praises of his fathers the sky light-
ened and the red turned to shimmering strands of pink and
then to pale flaky clouds in a blue sky behind the brilliant sun.

Later, he went to say good-bye to his sister, who was lying
alone in her hut, which had developed the thick, peculiar smell
of sickness and decay. She had lost hope of being cured after
the prophet had failed, but the disease itself seemed neither
worse nor better. Though she was younger than Mputuya, she
looked infinitely older—a bundle of wrinkled skin and fragile
bones covered in a dirty grey blanket. Only her eyes were alive,
and when he said good-bye they were full of pain and anxiety.

"It is heavy work that you have, my brother. Look after
yourself and do not let the place of Goli harm you."

"I will try to return as usual, my sister."

Her eyes grew hard and her voice cruel. "If you see him, you
know whom, tell him I never want him to come back."

"As you say, Sister," he boomed gently through the half-dark
room.

"Take my hand, my brother." She put her shrivelled hand in
his and they clasped thumbs. "Go well, Brother."

"Stay well, Nabo Timba."

He paid a farewell visit to the chief; finding Mpisi with him,
he greeted them both with more than usual courtesy, for when
one is going far away, into a place of danger, it is not wise to
show enmity. Mhau sent Mpisi to bring some beer, and the men
drank from one bowl.

"So you are taking your son with you, my friend," the chief
remarked conversationally.

Mputuya's big lips broadened, but it was a grimace rather

than a smile. "I'm not taking him with me, *Nkosi*. I am taking him away from me."

The chief looked puzzled.

"Yes, *Nkosi*," the father explained sombrely. "To me it is clear. I have worked all my life, and have got nowhere, and know nothing that my fathers did not know before me. Only one thing more I have learnt, and that is to be a servant of the white man, to dig for him and sweat for him and be despised by him. This is not what I want for my one remaining child. I want him to learn the reason why the whites are on top, and I think this may be found in the white man's books. And when he knows, I want him to teach others, so that our people can also be on top." A little warily, he said, "I tried to explain this at the meeting before my case, but you didn't seem to understand."

"Now, too, I don't understand," said the chief with a helpless gesture. "What must he know? What must he teach? Ploughing, or teaching, or just books?"

Mputuya's face crumpled in concentration, and only the scar looked smooth and clear, and he spoke hesitatingly. "That I don't know myself yet. But I think they must all be joined together."

"Will he earn big money that way?" queried Mpisi.

Mputuya shook his head. "That, too, I don't know. Perhaps —" and there was a gleam of malice in his eye, though his voice remained courteous—"perhaps his relations will help him if he is in need."

Old Beta ambled along, and asked Mputuya why he was leaving so soon. He disapproved of a man's leaving home to earn money to send a son to learn nonsense.

"A man seems to long to return to Goli after he has been there many times," Mpisi commented sourly, and Mputuya agreed: "Perhaps it is like a battle; once you are in it, you can't turn your back on the enemy."

They talked and drank, and drank and talked. Mputuya felt warm and mellow as he walked home in the late afternoon, stopping to chat to the chief's wives returning with faggots from the hills, and to a few friends back from a beer-drink.

Always, before he left the country, he wondered how he could leave the peace and quiet. When he reached the highest point on his road, he paused and gazed around. The hills in the distance were familiar and dear, and the little clusters of huts seemed part of the solid earth itself. The stalks from the fields gave out a faint nutlike smell and the setting sun glinted blindingly on the broad curve of the river.

When he came home, the boys were already milking. Timba, with a bright pheasant's plume in his mop, was busy tying together the legs of the brindled Siti Deep while Feka waited with the wooden pail between his legs. "Quiet, beautiful one." Timba's voice was one proud caress. "Siti Deepi, Siti Deepi, quiet." This cow had been named for the gold mine City Deep, on the Witwatersrand, where Mputuya had earned the money for her purchase.

Mputuya watched his son suck the first milk straight into his mouth before squeezing a thin, pure gush into the pail. This was the best time of day. When the boys had milked enough, they let in the calves to suckle, and the cows lowed contentedly and each licked its own calf with a rough but loving tongue. After the boys had taken the milk to the store-room, they ate the special dish of monkey nuts and dry porridge that the mothers had prepared and drew down the calabash of sour milk; having removed the stopper so that the grey-white whey spilt out, they shook the solid curd into a dish and ate until they could eat no more.

"I will remember this," said Feka contentedly, "when they give me the bad food that Potopoto's sons said they always cook at boarding-schools."

Back in their hut, they talked till late into the night. Timba was as excited as Feka at the great adventure that lay ahead, and only regretted that he would not be able to write, himself, in reply to the letters Feka would be writing home. Feka said, "The girl will do it for you."

A pause.

"Timba."

"Yes."

"I'd like to say good-bye to her again before I leave. Let us try to see her tomorrow."

So early in the morning they went down to that part of the river where the girls of Mhau's family drew water. From some way off Feka recognized Lamtana, and he said with a nervous laugh, "I am shaking."

The girls crowded round him, eager to wish him success, but the faithful Timba managed to divert Lamtana's companions for a few minutes while Feka spoke to her alone.

"Do not forget me. I will write to you, and please, *Mntan'-enkosi*, I beg reply."

The familiar words made the warm blood darken her skin, and she looked away.

"Lamtana," he pleaded. "I am going so far away."

"Yes. I will reply."

"I will remember you."

"Go well, Feka."

"Stay well, Lamtana."

Formally they shook hands. The boys left, and the girls shouted merrily, "We will meet again."

He found it saddest to say good-bye to his mother. She tried to stay her tears, "lest they weaken him on his road," but her eyes were wet. She gave him a little bundle of food for the journey and, taking his hand, muttered, "Let me kiss you, my child." She pressed her lips twice against his wrist in the old traditional way, and blew softly through the corner of her mouth.

"Go well, my son."

"Stay well, Mother."

**117**

"Look after things, my wife," said Mputuya gruffly.

Timba accompanied them to the bus stop. He walked behind, proudly carrying Feka's new box on his head; in front of him walked Feka with his father's belongings wrapped in a small bundle. Mputuya strode behind, carrying his stick. They sat at the roadside to wait patiently for the bus. The sun moved slowly overhead, shining brightly on the silver buttons of Feka's new blazer. For the last time Mputuya picked out the familiar sights, but Feka, with a rapt expression on his face, dreamed of things beyond the horizon, and Timba played idly with his herd-boy's pipe, on which he blew an occasional melancholy tune.

From the top of the ant heap, Lamtana waited until, in the late morning, the bus to Mbabane came thumping along, and she saw a tall man and a tall boy climb into the back. "I will write you in my thoughts, Feka."

Lamtana's interest in education germinated in the minds of a few of Mhau's younger children; they listened to her stories of wonders beyond the fables told by grannies, and asked to be allowed, also, to go to school.

Though it is hard to think that Sicenga was jealous and wanted to counteract Lamtana's influence, she undoubtedly felt sad that the children were prepared to leave her for books and chairs. So she decided, after lengthy discussions with Totwa, that it would be an excellent idea to organize an *umcwasho,* a traditional "growing-up" ceremony in which the children of the chief took precedence.

For this the queens gave full consent. Even Nabo Lamtana could see no catch in it: though it might be described as Sicenga's *umcwasho,* she knew the three girls would share the power equally, and, she conceded, it might even be quite profitable in cash.

Nabo Sicenga had never regretted brewing the beer for the first school uniforms, even though Sicenga had never worn one, but she had decided that she need not repeat the preliminaries for Velapi, now a chubby toddler who already strongly resembled her noble father.

When the wives approached Mhau as potential patron, he promised to provide all the cattle necessary to feast the participants.

Only Lamtana showed little enthusiasm for the whole idea, and put forward the extraordinary argument that the missionaries might object. Nabo Sicenga's thick, soft lips flattened into a tight line as she replied, "They will have no law to stop it. The *umcwasho* is our custom to make girls grow up sensibly. It is better than school. Girls are taught real knowledge, they learn they are women, not books."

Nabo Totwa laughed mischievously. "Let them object. We won't force the school children to join us. They'll just want to, by themselves."

She was right. The news of the princesses' *umcwasho* soon spread, and, on the opening, judiciously organized for a weekend so as not to interfere with school attendance, girls from all parts of the district flocked to the chief's village. They were all gay and carefree, and in their brightest clothes, and soon a crowd of cheerful and admiring youths gathered to watch the goings-on. But the girls would have nothing to do with them. They turned on them their shiny and colourful backs, and if a girl were addressed directly she replied with a disdainful jibe.

The senior princesses and a few special friends discussed the details of organization, occasionally seeking advice from the mothers, who looked on with amusement and pride. On Lamtana's recommendation, they appointed Tina as chief helper, that same spare-toothed girl who had read so well in front of the inspector.

The first thing to be done was to divide the girls into two groups, those old enough to have lovers, and those who were not yet old enough. Of the chief's children, Sicenga, Lamtana, and Totwa alone qualified for the senior grade; the others were Not-yets.

"This division," Totwa remarked to Lamtana, "is much simpler than the schoolteacher's counting of years"—and, she might have added, rather more accurate.

Classification completed, a suitable uniform had to be created, and the girls decided on simple modifications of the traditional courting dress. Sicenga commented that this was not nearly as expensive as, and even more beautiful than, any dress cut for school. It consisted mainly of copper buttons sewn on to a skirt made of a piece of black cloth six inches wide and bordered with a pattern of red and black china beads. From the right side of the skirt dangled colourful woollen tassels, of which the variety of hues distinguished the Old-enoughs from the Not-yets. The rest of the body was bare, but for a seductive band of multi-coloured woollen threads slung across the right shoulder and under the left breast; to this band the girls were permitted to tie match-boxes, bright gold and silver safety pins, and other decorations. This costume was to be worn in its entirety on all possible occasions, but scholars during school attendance were exempt.

To keep their identity, even when not in uniform, the organizers laid down special greetings and responses. Instead of saying, "We see you," an *umcwasho* girl had to quote curtly, "I say nothing," and instead of "Stay well," she was to dismiss the intruder with an aloof "Do not touch me." But the most important law, the one which carried the heaviest penalty, prohibited love-making by, or to, an *umcwasho* girl. "For touching, five shillings; for sleeping, an ox." On hearing this announcement the youths looked dismal, indeed, but the girls yelled gleefully,

"Oh, we hear, *Mntan'enkosi,* eh, eh, eh!" The *umcwasho* was to last an entire year from the formal opening, with full uniform, in two moons' time.

Before returning to their homes with this glad news, the girls, led by their own Lysistrata, went in a solid, singing phalanx to do service for her noble parents. Armed with enormous, gleaming knives, they marched down to the river where the tall reeds stretched graceful feathery heads. Plunging in boldly, the girls cut the brittle stems with sharp, effective strokes, till each had a bundle in tribute to the chief, from which his wives could build new reed fences for privacy. When the girls returned to Mhau's homestead, they flung their bundles down with songs and a flourish, and the chief himself came out of his hut and looked on approvingly.

On Monday Lamtana went to school, envying Sicenga and Totwa, who had been commissioned to buy the necessary materials from Simon's, but pride prevented her from accompanying them or expressing any regret.

For the next few weeks every homestead where there were unmarried daughters was enlivened by gossip and a busy sewing, in the spare time, of beads and buttons and match-boxes. On clear, moonlit evenings, the initiates came together to practise gay *umcwasho* songs, some old favourites and others new compositions. The best hit was a catchy little song by Totwa:

> "Oh the obstinate ones.
> What will the chief do to them?
> Hit them. Hit them.
> In school they teach papers.
> Hit them. Hit them.
> In *umcwasho* they teach laws.
> Hit them. Hit them.
> Oh the obstinate ones.
> Hit them. Hit them.
> *Shi shi shi.*"

The last match-boxes were stuck on the bands for the main day, which, again out of consideration for the scholars, had been set for a week-end.

"What a row!" Lamtana complained, as the visitors poured in, blowing on whistles more usually associated with police, and shouting and singing in loyal exuberance.

"It's lovely!" gloated Totwa. "Can you smell the food prepared for us all?"

At noon, Sicenga led the girls to the space in front of the chief's cattle byre to dance and parade themselves before a crowd of interested spectators. Mhau's eyes passed proudly but briefly over his own daughters standing in one long radiant line; they rested, with more than paternal interest, on a big girl of outstanding shape, and from her they roved and stayed on a lithe and smiling creature with a dreamy smile. It was several years—he counted four, to be exact—since he had taken a new wife, and he considered it wise to add at intervals that were not too great to make adjustment easy. He sent Mpisi to make the necessary enquiries as to the parentage of the two maidens whom he found so pleasing, and the more he watched, the more he wished the *umcwasho* had different rules.

He was not the only one, but he exercised more self-control than many; also, he had more compensations than most.

As the *umcwasho* went on, marked by the unforgettable maddening moonlight nights with the girls dancing, singing, dancing, the amount of fines, both in shillings and in oxen, soared. The princesses grew more arrogant, the youths more wary, the encounters more secret.

The chief's three oldest daughters were observed by all. Totwa was the most popular, and as she danced she looked at the boys with laughter-loving eyes that drove them reckless with desire to approach and grab her. But let them try. She looked at them again, shrewdly. She herself would choose soon; they could not hurry her. The old connoisseurs watched Lamtana, a golden beauty with supple waist, and firm hips and solid thighs, but eyes too searching for peaceful satisfaction. Sicenga was calm, ready to judge fairly by the standards she herself had accepted from ancient teaching.

School holidays brought Feka back from the city in the middle of it all. Down to the trysting place at the river he hurried the morning after his return, ignoring Timba's warning as a joke, ignoring everything in his excitement at the memories stored in his heart. Lamtana knew he was back, and where he would be, and longed to meet him alone. But girls stuck to each other like leeches, their eyes gimleting each other's evasions. Finally she decided it was better to see him in their presence than try to see him in secret.

It was a Saturday, and recklessly she announced that she was going to bathe; a chorus supported her, and off they all tripped. He saw them approach and, smiling foolishly in happiness, he came to greet them.

Lamtana shouted warningly, "We say nothing. Ha, ha."

He was no longer a timid boy from Swaziland. He had tasted city life. He swaggered up to them. He would just grab her breast in joke. His eyes were on her and on her alone. Realizing the danger, she tried to turn and run. The other girls blocked her way, and as he caught her, they were on him like vultures, croaking, "You touched her. You touched a princess. Pay."

The smile faded from his open mouth at the harshness of their voices and the mercenary gleam in their eyes. He dropped his empty hands. "What did you say?" he appealed to Lamtana.

"We say nothing." The voice was cruelly cold. He had made a fool of her.

"We said pay."

"Pay five shillings."

"Pay."

"Five shillings." They screamed in cackling chorus at their prey.

He wanted to shut his ears. "I haven't it." He shouted desperately.

124

"Get it."

"Get it quickly."

"Hurry."

The leader was Tina, his old schoolmate. He tried to smile at her. "I've just come home. Is this the way to greet me?" Cunningly, "I brought things from Goli. Presents."

"We don't want them. Don't you know this is *umcwasho?*" Enticingly, she mocked, "Five shillings for touch. A cow for sleep. Pay, or do you want me to call the others?"

"No. No." The hot shame made him almost dumb.

"Well?"

"I will find it."

"Go." They dismissed him.

"Hurry."

He did not look at Lamtana, but rushed off, his chest thumping. He had saved two shillings from the occasional pence his father gave him at school, and with this he had meant to buy sweets, lots of them, with words. It served her right not to get them.

His mother would hear and reproach him; he was glad his father was still at the mines. He sought out Timba, who was absorbed in the making of a new bird trap, and all the time that Feka spoke he kept on working. Only at the end he said, "You are lucky that the others were with her. If you had been caught alone together, you'd have had it. They'd all surround you and dance like hyenas, yelling songs to shame you." He shuddered. "I saw it once. Now if I hear the whole gang approaching, I run away." He laughed suddenly. "It's better, though, if you see it done to someone else, my brother. You are damned lucky."

Yes, Feka realized that. But he was still three shillings short.

At Timba's suggestion he went to Simon's straight away to ask for work; Simon, it seemed, had been helping many a boy in a similar predicament by giving employment for a few days with five shillings as the pay.

Simon wagged his finger at Feka. "Who is the girl?"

Feka hesitated. What business of his was it? The old goat. But his money was needed. Besides, he'd hear sooner or later. "Lamtana Nkosi Dlamini."

"Whew. You've got cheek," Simon said with a slight twinge of jealousy, and he wondered, as he had often wondered, why he himself had never tried to touch Lamtana. Perhaps, he decided, it really was because she reminded him of his Lomusa— and yet was so unlike that gentle, loving girl. So he nodded at Feka. "All right. Start on Monday, and I'll help you out. Pay five shillings a week."

"Five shillings a week?"

"Yes. I'm helping you. Don't think that because you go to school I must pay five shillings a day. What do you learn at school that can help me? Nothing. Do you want the job or not?"

"O.K."

"O.K. Monday early."

As Feka expected, his mother had heard, and shouted at him for wasting himself at his age first by chasing girls and then by working for nothing for Simon. But she was even more scathing about the mercenary nature of the modern girl; fancy asking five shillings just for touch. She told him how, in her day, the highest fine for that was a plaited grass bracelet or, at most, a sixpence. Of Simon she said contemptuously, "He plays with us. White people think we can eat for nothing." But she let Feka work, all the same—it would teach him—and for the rest of his holidays she found many tasks to occupy him. He did not once manage to see Lamtana alone, though whenever he could he loafed around with the boys and watched for her.

Mputuya learned of his son's misbehaviour on his return a few months later and was angry that it should have been with the chief's daughter, but to him the *umcwasho* was the play of children, not to be treated too seriously. Nor did the news that Mhau was negotiating with the parents of two of the girls surprise him, remembering how often his friend had spoken over this question and told Mputuya that he was foolish to be satisfied with only one wife. This time, too, Mhau broached the subject, arguing that if it were jealousy that Mputuya feared, he should get his wife to do the choosing. He himself never brought in anyone new without consulting Nabo Sicenga, who was always most sensible and co-operative. Mputuya said he would think about it, but he had too many other things already on his mind.

"What?"

School fees had been increased, his wife needed clothes, the gardens were neglected.

"A young and strong woman might help."

Mputuya dismissed the chief's suggestion. He was quite glad to return to the mines, after three months' rest and just before the *umcwasho* festivities were over.

By the time Feka arrived home for his next holidays, the whole district was in a state of joyous excitement. The Old-enoughs were on the march for lovers, but the princesses had to be more discreet than others and could not publicly proclaim their choice, though Timba confided sadly to Feka that everyone knew that Totwa had already committed herself to a warrior in a regiment that already had the king's permission to marry. "The other two daughters of the chief are still looking."

This time Feka waited a whole day before seeking out Lamtana. He had written two letters and received no answer, and he went the first morning to Simon's to find out if she had fetched them.

"Ha, ha," laughed Simon. "She learnt them by heart all right."

Feka felt so happy that, in spite of everything that had happened, he bought a bag of sweets and tucked them out of temptation deep in his pocket.

The next morning he was at the river. He waited till past midday, and she didn't come. Desolate, he went to Timba and stayed with him in the pasture-lands, and helped bring back the cattle and milk. The moon was up, and the two boys strolled together to the chief's village, from which came the sound of singing. The rest of the world seemed peacefully asleep; only a few invisible night creatures stridulated and squeaked, and the river frogs croaked their drinking songs.

Feka and Timba went to the barracks, where they had their friends, and from where they sat they could watch the girls. Most of them were dancing as they sang, but Lamtana was sitting apart playing the *isigubo,* striking the string softly with a fine reed and pressing the open mouth of the gourd against her breast, which served as resonator. As she played, she sang, and Feka strained to hear. It was a short song, shaped wistfully and sadly, and the girl filled the words and tune with melancholy passion. She was different from all others, he thought. Others would sing the same tune and the same words, but yet the song would never be the same. Everything about her was different, every movement full of strangely troubled and restless beauty.

After a time, while the others were still singing and dancing, she slipped away, not stealthily, but driven by her own thoughts, and as she went she saw him. Or perhaps she heard him, though he had not spoken her name. She gazed at him a long time and then went into her hut.

He was at the river only a little before her the next day, and his heart drummed loudly to the light tripping of her small, bare feet.

He greeted her stiffly, balancing his body as though to run, and she stood straight opposite him, bewitching him with her full young beauty.

After a long time spent in the formalities, she said, "Let us sit," and since she had not mentioned their unhappy previous encounter, he grew more courageous.

But this time he wooed her gently, pleading, "Let me taste your sweetness. There is no girl whom I have seen whom I wanted like you."

At first she would only play with him like a girl, but she

realized that he had become a man. And then he said urgently, "Lamtana, I promise you that in Goli they say what we are doing is uncivilized. [He used the English word.] It does not help you."

He had learnt much. She became weak with longing and curiosity. "Don't hurt me," she begged as she felt his hands push her down to the sun-spotted ground, and she looked into eyes deep black, bright, and hungry. "Don't spoil me."

"No," he whispered back.

When he had done, he sat up and said awkwardly, "Are you all right?"

"Yes." She lay very still, and he waited for her to speak. "Now go."

So he left her. After a while she washed herself in the river and the water was clean and very cold, and she scraped her body with a roughly rounded pebble till it felt raw and tingling. She pulled on her dress, trying to iron out the crumples with the palms of her hands. Gaily she sauntered home.

Sicenga and Totwa rushed to meet her accusingly. "Where have you been? Why are you so late? We searched everywhere for you."

"I was hot and had a headache and bathed in the river."

"Alone?"

"What are you saying to me, Sicenga?"

"We asked. Were you alone?"

"Of course. Now mind your own affairs. I have a headache."

She found no time to visit the Simons; they would be there when Feka again left her behind.

She never tired of questioning him about the city, yet somehow her knowledge was greater than his own, and when she talked she filled old familiar things with new meaning. He did not try to contain his pleasure in all she was, and it did not occur to him that he did not really know her. For she was never the same; usually she was eager, gay, and glowing, but suddenly and unaccountably she would seem remote, almost cold, and silent. He could never break through her real silence, though she responded with words to his questions. She seemed to be examining her inner mind, or listening to what he said and delicately pulling it apart to see if it were meaningful. Then she might grow impatient and play with him, her eyes dark and limpid as he sought to find himself in her. Again the holidays ended, and this time he left with deep sadness.

But she was surprised to find that she missed him less than before. The bodily longing was great, but she had built a more complete world into which she could escape, and of which he was not always part. In fact, she was oddly alone, and when the gaps in her new world needed filling she went to Simon's. Her "Book of Thots" was nearly full, and on the last page she wrote: "The truth is like the hart. It cannot be seen. My Boy frend is gone, but I do not feel my tears. I have in me the bite of hunger, but it is not for meat but for learning."

The visiting missionary fulminated from the pulpit of the schoolroom, his voice emanating from a thin neck that rose like rubber tubing from the hard white collar. His head swayed this way and that, and his eyes rolled round the congregation.

"I am shocked and horrified, but not surprised"—his hand raised in denial of surprise—"by the effects of this immoral heathen custom, the *umcwasho*"—the word spoken like squasho —"on our young people. The Christian virtues of chastity and purity have been debased by girls and boys whom we hoped to lead in the path of righteousness. Must we Christians follow the disbelievers parading in primitive finery? Or must we denounce them? We, my brethren, must denounce them. Their sin is obvious. It is our duty to God to point the finger of shame at—"

from a list he read each name like a death knell—"at Bell Nkosi, Maria Zwane, Josephine Hlophe, Angeline Nkosi, Daisy Motsa. . . ." Solemnly he tolled twenty chimes of doom. "These," he continued lugubriously, "once respected members of our church, are temporarily excommunicated, and we, we remaining few,"—and few, indeed, they were—"must struggle on alone. Yet not alone. For God is with us. And let the sinners seek forgiveness with true penitence, that He in His infinite goodness may forgive them for the sake of the children soon to be born. For Jesus our Lord does not punish the innocent with the guilty."

The congregation, consisting entirely of women and sadly depleted by the absence of all unmarried girls bar one, Miss Emily Sibanze, listened with apparent meekness to the sermon and, since it was delivered entirely in English, interpreted it as best they could; from tones and gestures (especially the pointing finger of shame, a very rude gesture and indicative of evil), they gathered that the missionary was sadly displeased. Miss Emily Sibanze, who had evoked not a single fine during the entire *umcwasho,* was conscious of the glances of hostility from women shrewd enough to guess who had supplied the white man with the names of the erring.

Post-*umcwasho* babies were not restricted to "mission" girls, but it was clear to all except the missionaries that the non-Christian girls had been more careful. Following tradition, the Old-enoughs had considered it both right and proper to take lovers at the end of the *umcwasho,* but, also following tradition, they accepted that pregnancy was beyond the limit.

The princesses in particular were advised to be circumspect, and the mothers spoke openly in their presence of the dangers as well as the joys of girlhood. Discussing the matter with her sisters, Totwa confided that she was having trouble with her Singani, a gallant-looking man who did not wish to appear unappreciative of the permission granted his regiment to reproduce.

"He is so strong," she added, "and can look so sad that it is hard to refuse."

Sicenga sympathetically suggested additional caution, but Lamtana asked what he said and did, and having listened with unusual interest to Totwa's detailed report, commented, "He does not seem to me so hard to resist." She did not talk to them of Feka.

For three months after he left, she was quite happy, and not until her sisters, acquainted with the intimate rhythm of her life, began to question her did she grow anxious about herself. "Perhaps," she thought hopefully, "I am sick without feeling sick." But then her mother commented that her school dress was getting tight, and was about to make some further remark when she stopped short and looked again. The swanlike neck jerked back. Was it the light, or had Lamtana's complexion changed in some subtle way? The head bent forward. The slim waist seemed unusually round, the hips more full. She put the direct question. Lamtana denied it. Her mother did not really believe her, but decided to wait.

A few days later, interrupting a conversation between the two other senior wives, who were clearly embarrassed by her entry, Nabo Lamtana demanded, "What are you whispering about?"

"Oh, nothing. We were just talking."

"What about?"

"Children."

"Well?"

Bravely, Nabo Sicenga faced her. "Your daughter is with stomach?"

"How do you know?"

"We see and we hear."

It is never easy for a proud and quick-tempered woman to accept humiliation with dignity, yet Nabo Lamtana controlled herself and said almost quietly, "Yes. This is a thing that no one can hide from others. I saw it and hid it from myself; she saw it and hid it from herself; but when you saw, because she is not yours you did not hide it. No matter, it will soon be public to all."

To them she did not condemn her daughter, but alone with Lamtana in the hut she showed no restraint. She beat her across her head, face, and body and insulted her with every filthy name she knew. Lamtana cowered and cried, and could neither excuse nor explain. Yet she felt no shame, only fear and anger. She knew what to expect. The old wives with their searching, bleary eyes, seeing the present through a film of past pretences; the younger women whom *lobola* had made respectable gossiping with lewd tongues; the bachelors made bolder by desire tinged with a new promise. If only she could escape. But where? At the moment there was no escape. She bit her tongue to stop herself from screaming back at her mother.

The chief had already settled the matter of the two new young wives very satisfactorily, and when Nabo Sicenga informed him of his daughter's condition he shouted, in rage more feigned than felt, "This comes from schooling. I told you it ruined girls. Who is the boy? I'll make him pay."

On learning that it was the son of Mputuya, he roared himself into a louder and more genuine fury.

"A bull calf without horns ruining the children of his father's best friend." And he denounced Feka roundly as a boy without respect or sense of duty, prepared to make his father pay while he indulged himself in school pleasures. His father would have to pay two beasts for damages; his, Mhau's, daughter was no common girl.

Old Beta fanned the flame. Feka belonged to the Locust Regiment, which had not yet been given permission by the king to marry. That would make an extra fine of a beast to the king himself. The young rogue, emptying his father's cattle byre for his pleasure.

And Mpisi ostentatiously pitied Mputuya, who was working so hard to educate the boy.

All this was reported to Nabo Lamtana, whose anger against her daughter became more intense. In Lamtana's condition the mother saw her own decline; the two girls whom the chief had brought into the harem were Lamtana's age. Since they had been brought to the chief, he had paid little attention to Nabo Lamtana; she wanted to beat them, revile them, drive them out. But over them she had little power; they, and Nabo Sicenga, were on guard. She tormented Lamtana instead.

She dragged her to Feka's mother, who was at first too confused to speak, one half of her rejoicing, "I will have a grandchild," and the other half bemoaning, "My son has spoilt the chief's child."

Politely, but not unkindly, she spoke. "I do not say the girl is lying, but I must hear what my son says, too. I will write to him and his father, and when the child is born we will see the truth more clearly."

Lamtana snapped, "The truth is here."

"I see it, girl," said Feka's mother gently. "We will not deny a child of my son."

Timba's mother, whom Nabo Feka had called in, shuffled closer. "And the young wife of the son would be welcome in this house of old people."

Nabo Lamtana turned on her viciously. "I will never agree to let my child come to a place where it is common for women to be abandoned by their men. Does that boy think, when he will run to the town for pleasure, Lamtana will have brothers to look after her? You should know what happens to women who are tricked by a man of Goli. What has turned you into the thing you are?"

The sick woman, deeply wounded, replied, "As you say, I am just a thing," and drew herself back into the protection of the hut wall. But Feka's mother could not let her husband be insulted by anyone, even a senior wife of the chief, and replied strongly, "You should be glad to have your daughter with child of our home, for my husband has never abandoned one of his kin, no matter how sick or useless. And he will see that a child of his child is cared for, and the mother with it."

But Lamtana found herself thinking with pain, "I can't come here. I don't want to live here. I don't care if they do want me. Or how many cattle they give for me. This is not my place." The two women were old, dried out, further from her than the mothers she knew. The men, Mputuya, Feka, Timba, would be outside, free; she would be the young wife, handmaiden to the two old women. What would become of her thoughts and hopes?

On the way back she did not listen to her mother's obscenities and her insults to Feka's family, but she knew that at least in one respect her mother would be on her side; she would not willingly consent to her going as wife to Feka's home.

After they had left, Feka's mother walked to the schoolhouse and dictated two short letters, setting out the facts as she had been told them.

Miss Sibanze, as scribe, clucked, "Lamtana and Feka. No wonder she had stayed away from school these last weeks. And to think I hadn't noticed. I trust too much. It is a pity they don't belong to our church. They could both have been excommunicated as sinners."

Feka's mother did not ask how that would help; she was wondering a little guiltily why she couldn't think of them as sinners and why, if they were, she felt so happy, and she only hoped that Mputuya would not be too angry.

His reply came quickly and she was distressed that he should say, "Your news killed me." The letter went on, "It is true. I have seen our son, and he agreed. He wept tears." Was this a thing for tears? The letter ended, "I have still three months to my join. Don't do anything till I return."

Feka did not write to his mother, but to Lamtana, who had not been to the trader's for a couple of weeks. When Simon sent word to her that a letter had arrived, she came in considerable agitation to fetch it. Finding Simon engaged, she took it herself from the tray where he kept the post and, not waiting to reach home, opened it immediately. Tears flooded her eyes as she read, "Dear *Nkosatana*. That news from my mother made me lose my sense. Why did you not write to me yourself? Why did you complain first to my mother? Is it truly my child?" When she read this, she could go no further. She stifled sobs of hurt and humiliation. The formal opening. The indignant, unworthy accusation. She felt she never wanted to see him again. She did not even feel she wanted to explain that she had tried to write after the visit to his mother, and that for once she had lacked the right words. How could she tell him her reaction to the two women? The possessiveness of the mother? The decay and disease of the aunt? She had to talk to someone, and went stumbling to Mrs. Simon.

Mrs. Simon had heard the gossip from her husband, and was waiting eagerly for a visit from the girl whose company she had missed more than she had expected, and for whom the machine provided a poor substitute. When she saw Lamtana she greeted her warmly and was about to reproach her for neglect, when she noticed how timidly the girl responded. She stood in the doorway in her tight dress, looking young and helpless, her eyes wide with pain, the letter crumpled in her hand.

The trader's wife said simply, "Sit, my friend," addressing the girl for the first time with the term of true equality. "Sit and talk to me of your trouble." The genuine tenderness and concern in her voice made Lamtana turn to her pleadingly and hand her the letter.

While Mrs. Simon read it, tears rolled down Lamtana's cheeks and she wiped them clumsily with her hand, and she went to the door and blew her nose between her fingers and was more unhappy and awkward than any human being Mrs. Simon had seen, so that she did not know what to say, but read and reread the letter until Lamtana was more herself. Then Mrs. Simon said wisely, "He is afraid, for he is still young."

But this started Lamtana again. "I, too, am young and afraid," she sobbed.

When Mr. Simon came in, he found the two women weeping. Embarrassed, he laughed loudly, then coughed and said heartily, "Is someone dead? No! Then there's nothing to cry about."

His wife looked at him reprovingly and gave him the letter. He read it, and then, in a voice more quiet than usual, said something Lamtana never forgot. "If all goes well, he should be proud, not afraid," and his little eyes shone and his nose had a different, redder tinge.

Lamtana's visits to Mrs. Simon again became frequent, till malicious tongues whispered that she had reason for going there, and her mother, to whom this was hinted by one of the young wives, told Lamtana with blazing eyes to stop wandering around like a white man's prostitute. Stunned and horrified by this additional injustice, Lamtana stayed away from the two people who showed her the kindness and affection denied her in her own home.

Mputuya returned, slightly more gaunt than usual, and above the scar a patch of hair had gone greyish-white. When he spoke to the chief, he held himself in reserve, and even though the chief tried to show him friendship and said he blamed only the boy, Mputuya replied stiffly as through a mask clamped over his face, exposing only his eyes. In them the chief read unexpressed accusation, and he listened resentfully to Mputuya's spoken words. He had come back this time with enough cash for one beast, and the other he would take from his herds. He identified it. Siti Deep, the brindled beauty, the herd-boy's pride, a trophy from a past battle in one of the deepest mines.

Mpisi asked, "Why not give both beasts from those you already have, and keep the money? The price of cattle has gone up since you left."

Mputuya did not even look at him. He was not worth it. Didn't he understand that it was easier to pay a fine with a beast you didn't know than to part with one that was already part of you?

He moved on to his next point of discussion with the chief. When the child was born, he would bring further cattle to give it the father's family name, but he would prefer to give full *lobola* and get the mother as well. Would the chief accept fifteen head for her? He had the cattle and would gladly use them for this purpose. He knew these were matters their respective family councils would need to decide, but he would like to hear the chief's opinions.

Mhau, feeling remote from Mputuya, was not particularly anxious to discuss the matter and not rude enough to say so. "The girl's mother refuses," he apologized.

Mputuya's face remained vacant. "The girl will be cared for, *Nkosi,* and what she has done will not be to her shame, for she will have built the line of my father. I want my son's children." Then he spoke of the importance of children, with the terrible understanding of a man who has lost many and has one son, only one son, left.

But he did not beg and did not excuse his son. The chief listened without real sympathy. The situation was outside his experience of suffering.

Old Beta, angered by Mputuya's presumption in pressing a claim for a boy whose age group was not yet permitted by the king to marry, advised him dourly, "If you want more children, use your cattle for a wife for yourself, and not for your unfledged child."

Mhau thrust the point home. "Yes, age-mate. Haven't I often told you that you yourself are not too old?" And he laughed boisterously, his big body shaking with mirth.

"I hear, *Nkosi,*" said Mputuya soberly and soon took his leave. He would have liked to see the girl and speak with her, but custom forbade contact between him, the potential father-in-law, and her, the young and pregnant daughter-in-law. He would have liked to tell her himself that he, too, would be glad to have her in his home; not for a moment did he imagine that she might be unwilling to go there.

He instructed his wife to talk to the girl, and when she told him with some perplexity that she had received no response whatsoever from her, he calmed her. "She is right to behave this way. She is obeying her parents. We must wait for the child."

Timba, who tried to find out from Totwa and Sicenga what Lamtana really wanted, came back with the information that she would speak to no one about herself, and pretended nothing was wrong.

"She pretends she has no stomach," he said crudely, "only the blister of an elephant." He had grown taller and lankier and more restless these last months, and he was not quite as gay as before and complained that all girls were false.

Lamtana, now big and slightly clumsy in her movements, waited Feka's return, waited, not with tenderness and love, but with feelings too twisted for peace. She wanted to tell him how she hated him, but not by letter; she wanted to shout at him her rejection of his child and see him suffer. She longed for him and at the same time despised him. His letter had torn away her inner security, and she stopped writing down her thoughts.

The morning she heard he was back, she came openly to his home and went straight to the sleeping hut that he shared with Timba. The women saw her coming and looked at each other with delight, but did not show themselves. Feka's mother put a pan of monkey nuts to roast on the fire for her son to offer to the girl if she stayed, then, thinking she had no further part to play just yet, went to work her fields.

Lamtana found Feka sitting alone, looking through the things he had brought back in his now somewhat battered trunk. As she came in, he leapt up and over the box, and came to her with both hands out and his face illuminated with a big smile. Then he saw her looking at him as on the dreadful, unforgettable day of the *umcwasho,* and he dropped his hands and fumbled for something to say.

"How are you?" was all he could muster.

She spat at him. "You should know. You have made me as I am with your promises and lies," and she reviled him for saying he would not spoil her, and for what he had written in the letter, and screamed, "The child is yours. What you did to me you know and I know. You and you alone did it."

He was astonished by her rage and tried to placate her, admitting that the child was his and even claiming it. Then why had he written as he had? As though she were a loose girl of Goli. How many children had he made there, that he could think of her like that?

He tried to explain and defend himself. It had come as a shock, and he had been afraid of his father's anger.

She sneered at him. "Afraid. Always afraid of your father. Why not afraid of me and my father?"

He admitted that he had been afraid of them, too, but now he pleaded, his parents wanted her and the child. This was too much for Lamtana. They wanted her! But she didn't want them or him. She would never come to his home, and if they brought her by force she would run away.

She was standing there half-sobbing, and he sought to reach over to her, but she pushed him off, and as she was so differently shaped from before he was afraid to persist.

"Why did you come to my hut?" he asked, bewildered and uncomprehending.

"To shame you in your own home," she shouted, black eyes on fire and head high.

He, too, began to grow angry. What he had done was neither terrible nor unusual. She was obstinate for nothing. If she didn't want him, she could go, but the child was his. When it was born, that would be evident, and his father would give the cattle for it and get it whether she liked it or not, for that was the law.

As he ranted and boasted in the hut, she realized that he was really proud of his achievement. Like a young bull. He approached her again and this time she shoved him hard on the chest, so that he lurched back, but he jumped forward and caught both her arms and felt the exultation of his own strength as he gripped her and she was helpless.

No. She bit hard into his forearm and this time he struck her, so that she screamed loudly, and the sick woman crouching in the hut next door dragged herself as fast as she could to the door, shouting, "Leave off. Leave off."

As she crawled in and found them panting and struggling, she clutched the girl in her thin ropelike arms and, like a twisted creeper, bent over her in protection and yelled, "You stay off her."

Feka fell back, hot and babbling in wrath and excitement, and the girl shouted fresh insults. She wrenched herself free from Nabo Timba's stifling embrace and stumbled blindly along the path.

Feka, empty and frustrated, knew that she would go to their place near the river and bathe herself before returning home, and yet he dared not follow. He spent the day wondering and wishing he had not come home, and when his mother heard from Nabo Timba what she had seen and heard, she looked at him for the first time that he could remember with eyes hard and unloving and said bitterly, "If you have harmed my grandchild I will never forgive you."

Lamtana told nothing to her family of what had happened. All night she tossed on her mat in a turmoil of wrath, grief, rebellion, and fear till she felt she would go mad. Her feelings for Feka were all mixed up. She had gone there to shame him, as she had said, but he had claimed her and he had strength, and she no longer knew what she wanted. Her body was heavy and alive, and the world was unknown.

The child was born two days later in a store hut of Nabo Sicenga's, and according to that good woman, the birth "was easy enough, for all birth is pain."

The girl had tried to do everything for herself and, on waking long before dawn, had taken herself quietly out of the hut, but Sicenga had heard her leave and waited for her to return and, when she did not do so, decided to tell the mothers. Nabo Sicenga and Nabo Totwa had found her at the river and taken her back to the homestead. Together with others of the homestead, they held her down, and she bit into her lip to stop herself from screaming.

Nabo Sicenga encouraged her, "It is sweet to be with a man, but hard to bear. Strengthen yourself, or you'll weaken the child." Nabo Totwa gave her bawdy encouragement. Her own mother, following custom, did not come in till all was over, but it would not really have mattered if she had, since the reason given for the custom is that a mother's pity for her daughter might lessen the labour effort and harm the baby. As it was, the baby cried loudly at birth, and the women inside thrilled, "A boy to herd cattle," and they asked the name of the baby's father's clan, so that his identity would be known for all time, and Lamtana's voice was without shame as she spoke it.

For a week she remained indoors, and because she was the chief's daughter, Mpisi's wife was told to cook for her and tend her.

Lamtana began to feel a deep tenderness for the baby nestling close to her in waking and in sleep. On the seventh day, after she had been purified and allowed into the sunshine, Feka's mother brought a gift in brown paper, which the girl received in both hands but did not open; her eyes were unhappy, though her mouth gave thanks, and she did not show off her beautiful baby, wrapped in a little blanket, asleep on the ground beside her. This woman, this mother of Feka, would see soon enough that it was her son's son and would claim him.

The older woman sat watching without speech, and though she knew that by law the baby was still unimportant, a thing without human shape or name, which, if it died, would receive no proper burial, to her it was already a person, the first person her son had ever made.

On leaving, she said, "The cattle are there for you."

Lamtana made no reply. The old woman waited.

"Go well." Lamtana's voice was almost friendly.

"Stay well, young mother."

Lamtana did not know how much Feka himself wanted to hold his child, yet dared not come to the chief's home. Again he used Timba as his mediator, and Timba spoke to Totwa.

"He is full of pain that he must return to school without seeing her or the child. He has sent this letter."

"I will give it to her."

Lamtana read it. It was short. "Receive my letter, take it and keep it. I ask how you are. I have done you wrong truly. Now I want you and our child. I have no more excuse to make. Please, I beg reply. Good-bye, Dear [in English]."

She said to Totwa, "Tell him to write from Goli, then I will see."

With the help of Hlubi, the medicine man, the baby grew strong. He was smoked in thick, pungent-smelling medicines to ward off evil, and washed in foamy potions to make him shine, and he was shown to the moon, that all nature might be his friend. When it was finally seen that he would survive that first moon of danger, Nabo Sicenga named him Sipiwo, The Gift.

Lamtana sat in her hut, resting a new exercise book on the wooden trunk, and on the cover she printed "More Thots." She still mouthed the words as she wrote them down, and her spelling was not much improved, but her writing was more legible and the letters were firm and round.

On the clean front page she wrote, "He has gone back again. For years have passed since first he left. For years are a long time. They are maw than the lifetime of my child. Yet each time he riturns I forget the moons that he has been away. How grately he is lurnt now. He has past Standard VI and is pushing forwood with strength. It is hevy to be woman. We great ones are the eggs of the nation. We cannot help ourselves."

The child had apparently changed her life. She no longer

went to school and seldom wore Western dress, and she had her hair pulled, like her sisters', into a tight bun high on her head to show that she was officially marriageable. She worked regularly in the fields and conscientiously accepted the role of a chief's older daughter in the various ceremonies that punctuated the passing of the seasons. Little Sipiwo had been weaned after his second winter. He was plump and bright and lovable, and never lacked people willing to carry him or play with him. When he cried, they brought him to her and she fondled and caressed him.

But her innermost self remained untamed, wild and curious. When she visited the shop, which was more difficult because of the child, she talked of things beyond the boundaries of the district she knew, and in the quiet of the hut she continued to write her "Thots."

She refused to go to live at Feka's home despite the blandishments of his mother and, more difficult to resist, the pleading of Feka himself. She dreaded the idea of the old woman smearing her with the red clay of wifehood, after which she knew she would never again be free. Yet she was in love with Feka; when he was near she was happy, and when he was away at school she did not go to other men.

Mputuya had instructed his wife to keep an eye on her, but not to press her, only to remind her that by law they could claim the child when he was old enough, even if she refused to go to its father's home.

Sicenga and Totwa could not understand Lamtana any more than Feka's family could. If she were fond of Feka, why was she so determined not to go to his mother? And if she were not, why did she remain faithful to him alone?

Both of the girls were enjoying a very happy time, recognizing this as the most jolly and carefree period of their lives. They knew that sooner or later they would be married to men considered suitable by their father, men of responsibility and substance. Lamtana also knew this, and it was perhaps in dread of this that she had penned the proud and despondent words, "We great ones are the eggs of the nation. We cannot help ourselves."

She was startled by Totwa's voice calling her urgently. Hurriedly closing the book, which she thrust into the trunk, she came blinking into the sunlight, calling, "Here I am."

"What were you doing?"

"Nothing. Resting."

"You rest too much. You've done no work to make you tired today," complained Totwa with some irritation. "Since he left, you've done nothing but sit in the hut, 'resting.' "

"Do you have to work for me?" retorted Lamtana. "Do you feed my child?"

"Don't scold," said Totwa contritely. "I came to tell you some news." She dropped her voice. "Do you remember hearing of a chief from Twalitsha called Bomu?"

"Yes. Why?" Fear quivered through the question.

"He has sent to beg a bride."

"Swear."

"I swear by Father." Totwa put her finger into her mouth and ejected it with a plop.

"Who told you?"

With huge delight Totwa explained how she had seen four strangers arrive and speak to Mpisi, who after a while took them to her father. She thought at first it was simply another case coming to his court, but then the chief sent for some beer, and she had carried it in to the men. "As I came through the doorway, the leader—a man almost as big as Mputuya—was saying, 'And so, Father, we beg a fire.' I nearly dropped the pot."

"What was the reply?"

"Nothing definite. The family council will have to decide, of course."

Lamtana's voice trembled as she asked, "Whom do you think they will choose?"

"I'd choose Sicenga. But it may be you."

"If they choose me, I won't go." The words broke from Lamtana with uncontrollable passion.

Totwa's eyes widened. "You're crazy. Where will you find another handsome young chief?"

Lamtana repeated, "I won't go," adding with emphasis, "I'll run away. I'll complain to the white man."

Totwa struck her hands together in horror. "What are you saying?"

Lamtana said frantically, "I don't care. I hate Bomu."

"Shut up, Lamtana. You don't know him. You don't know what you are saying!"

With a wild, pathetic look, Lamtana turned to Totwa. "Would you go?"

"Of course, if our people said I should. Marriage is hard for women, but what can we do? It is the law. Anyway, now you know."

The messengers stayed for three days, and the purpose of their visit was common gossip, but no sign was made to the princesses as to which one of them would be given. The mothers, obviously excited, expressed general approval of Bomu, judging him from the character of his father, a great friend of Mhau's, as well as from rumours about the young chief himself. Sicenga accepted the possibility with her usual calm and when goaded by Totwa to express her opinion, said with her slow, warm smile, "Our elders will know best." Lamtana, after her first violent outburst, which Totwa repeated only to Sicenga, maintained a grim, burning silence.

Shortly after the messengers returned home, Mhau called together the family council, particularly the old men related to his father and his father's father. They came, withered men, lined with knowledge, deeply respected for their ancient wisdom, with memories like embalmed parchment on which every family event was imperishably entombed.

Mhau's wives bowed their heads before them, the great in-laws, and avoided them as much as possible. It infuriated Lamtana to see the mothers' humility. She felt an arrogant superiority that she would never have dreamed of expressing even to Totwa. To her, they appeared old, dirty men who could neither read nor write, who knew of nothing except their own customs and country, who were admired because they could repeat, and who condemned all new things and new thoughts. She despised everything about them—their clothes, their love of beer, their long stories of the past. But it was they who would decide her future. And at the same time as she despised, she feared.

She was not at home when they came to their decision. She had left Sipiwo with the other children and escaped to the Simons to talk over her dilemma. In her own mind she was sure that she would be selected. The more she considered the matter, the more certain it seemed. Bomu was not only one of the leading chiefs in the whole country, but an educated man; she alone would be his equal. Should she go? Could she refuse? And if she refused? What about Feka?

Mrs. Simon listened with her mouth full of pins and a deep frown seaming her forehead. In the end, she expressed herself in favour of marriage to the young chief, "For then you will be the big wife and will have others to work for you, and you can be proud, if dissatisfied, and come often on visits to your home."

But unexpectedly Simon said, "Go to the home of the father of your child, and if it gets too bad, leave."

"Leave? And then?"

"Then see," and he shrugged. "Come to me if you like."

She looked at him. He was kind but stupid. Stupid in a different way from the ancients in the kraal, stupid perhaps in a white man's way.

The old men were very observant. They noticed more than the women or children dreamed, and when they came together over the beer pot they discussed every detail of the treatment and impressions they had received. At last, Mhau broached the subject on which all the men had been pondering.

"Tell me, my fathers, which of my children should I send to be the wife of the chief of Twalitsha?"

Old Beta took a pinch of snuff, sneezing with pleasure, and then began. "For my part, the matter is quite clear. Three of the girls are ready for wifehood and any of them would be suitable. But she whom I would choose is Sicenga, the daughter of your first wife. From her mother she has learned a respect that will never shame you. The people of her husband's home will never go hungry. Like her mother, her hands are not idle and her heart is generous. She will bear children and teach them well without either spoiling them or breaking their bones. Of the girl of the third wife as well, I have but good to say. She would make any man laugh and treat him with kindness, but her heart is still too young to be tied firmly to one pole. Rather, let her go with her wildness for a time; but watch her well, or before you know she will be in trouble. As for the girl Lamtana, I know not what to say. The greatness of her birth equals that of the young chief who begs a bride. But her pride is greater even than that. She has learned much of new ways, and it will be hard to bring her back to the old. Never did I like your sending your children to school, my son, for there they learn little but contempt for old laws." Old Beta pulled in his head and drew down his right hand with a gesture of dismissal. "If you want to rejoice the young chief, therefore, I say give him Sicenga. If you want to be rid of trouble in your own home, send Lamtana."

There was a chorus of approval, and others contributed their opinions. Mhau listened carefully.

Lubelo spoke in his usual whining voice. "My brother, we great ones must always respect the blood, and so, though I agree with what our father Beta and the others have said, I want to make it clear that Lamtana is the one to send. Let Sicenga remain. Why break up the best of your own home for that of a stranger? When we come here, Sicenga rejoices our eyes, but the other avoids us, holding her head on high. When she must give us food, she does not place the sticks of honour on the top or bring us the bowl gladly; what the other does lingers sweetly on the tongue, so I say, my brother, send Lamtana."

Lubelo had undoubtedly made a point. Eventually, all turned to Mhau, who with dignified assurance spoke. "I have heard you now, my kinsmen, and I thank you. The sense of one man is like the strength of an ant, but joined with that of others it can make or destroy a village. My own heart pushes me along the road of Beta, my father. It is no service," he said, looking directly at Lubelo, "to my father's friend to send him the wild one from my own home. The dirt of one's hut should be hidden from strangers, not flung into their eyes. Lamtana worries me. What would she do to her husband? Her mother has spoiled her, and her head is full of school nonsense. For her I will find an old man who will hold her well."

Lubelo knew that it was useless to remonstrate and so concurred ingratiatingly. "I spoke only to stir your wisdom, my brother."

"Then," said Beta with a yawn, stretching himself fully, "the matter is settled."

Not one had mentioned the child, Sipiwo, though all knew of his existence; they took it for granted that if Lamtana were chosen, her Gift would remain behind at Mhau's till it was fetched by the father's family.

Mhau sent for Nabo Sicenga, and she came slowly, sensing why she was summoned even before Beta put the council's opinion to her.

"Mother of Sicenga, we see how well you have looked after your children, and now your eldest is ready to depart. A woman bears sons for herself, but daughters build up another's home. We do not force you to send her away, but the people of Bomu would care for her well."

Nabo Sicenga listened as the men spoke. She was very still and dignified, sitting alone on the woman's side of the hut facing the men, the power.

After they had spoken, she replied, "I thank you for the honour bestowed on me and on my daughter, who is a good girl, as you all know. A mother does not wish to see her child spoilt before marriage, nor does she like to see her power wasted; therefore it is well that a suitable husband has been found."

Sicenga was grinding grain when her mother returned and called her, and together they went to the mother's sleeping hut. "My child,"—Nabo Sicenga's voice was infinitely gentle—"you have grown up."

The girl's head was bent. "Yes, Mother."

"It is time for you to marry. Do you agree to our choice of the chief of Twalitsha?"

"I listen, Mother."

"It is well. We will prepare. That is all."

For a few minutes they remained in silence, sad at the prospect of impending separation, but resigned. Then Nabo Sicenga spoke with her usual serenity. "We must cook, my child." Slowly they walked outside.

Everyone, apart from Nabo Lamtana, was delighted with the choice, and though she said, "I am glad I will still have my child with me for a while," her disappointment was obvious from the way in which she twisted her lips and walked away from the other gossiping women.

Knowing how anxiously Lamtana was awaiting the decision, Totwa went along the path to the shop to meet her. Miss Sibanze had also been at the shop, and the two had returned together. Miss Sibanze was looking tight-lipped. She had found the journey very unprofitable, being quite unable to extract from Lamtana any interesting news from the chief's home. Nor did it make her feel more friendly when Lamtana, on seeing Totwa, almost pushed her over as she hastened towards her sister.

"What did they say?"

"It's all right, Sister. They chose the other one."

Lamtana turned a yellow-grey, and for a moment Totwa

seemed to sway in front of her and stars danced in her head. Then she steadied herself. "I have escaped." And she repeated this in a dead-calm voice to convince herself. Then she smiled, wildly happy and relieved, and thanked Totwa.

Miss Sibanze enquired acidly what all the haste was about, and Totwa said quite openly, "Sicenga is to marry Chief Bomu of Twalitsha."

"And why are you so happy?" Miss Sibanze probed Lamtana, whose face was suddenly radiant.

Totwa chuckled. "This time she has escaped."

Lamtana blinked. "This time," she echoed vaguely, and as they walked home those words kept on running through her head.

There were preparations throughout the district for the oncoming celebration. All the young still unmarried girls who had been in Sicenga's *umcwasho* were to join the bridal party and accompany the young princess going to wed the noble prince.

Tremulous excitement whirled through Mhau's home in soft pools of sexual power. Marriage, symbol of all things past and those to come. Each step laid down through distant ages. The new hair-style—the curls of girlhood pulled into the high pot-bun of womanhood. Tears for freedom lost. The light clothing of innocence discarded for the heavy skirt of soot-black hide and the goatskin apron. Brooms, mats, beads, rugs prepared, to win the strangers' hearts and show good intent. As time drew near, the big clay pots bubbled beer to speed the bridal party on its way, and the girls and youths—Timba, too—with ancient hags and smooth-tongued men to lead, swayed in practised dance through the moonlight nights. The ritual of departure marked by undulating bellow of the sacrificial ox. Gall from full bladder burnt mystic essence on Sicenga's mouth and tongue and virgin limbs, then the empty bladder, blown to phallic size, bound proudly on her head. The mother's parting tears, the bride's deep pain. Old flat-dugged women shrilled experienced advice. "Jealousy and suspicion will move at your side. Co-wives will accuse you of witchcraft. The man will beat you and you will submit. Children and pain will come."

Nabo Sicenga uttered words of motherhood. "Do not reply to evil tongues. Weep your tears alone, my child. Remember us at home and have courage. We do not abandon you. Farewell."

Mhau called down ancestral blessings. In the great shrine hut, with sunlight burning in moted flight from low-arched door to sacred hearth, "Tell them her virtues," he bade his deputies, "her strength of body and her docile nature. Look on her, my fathers, guard her with white eyes."

At last the party moved towards the setting sun, and from the earth itself seemed to rise the ancient song of Mhau's noble clan.

> "*Djia a o o dji a o o*
> "Hut of spears,
>   Blades of light.
> "*Djia o o dji a o o*
> "The light shines bright,
>   Hut of spears."

During the days on the road, food on big wooden platters came from humble folk as tribute to the great chief's daughter, and at night houses of friends were open while couples wandered forth into the fields. Lamtana, on waking, missed the warmth of Totwa from her side, but did not need to ask where she had been when, in the still enduring darkness, she returned her eyes bright with animated guilt.

They came to Bomu's village in the twilight, when ancestral gods rouse their dormant powers. The bridal party closed about Sicenga and danced her forward, hidden in their midst. Her soft, averted face stirred Bomu's pleasure. And there were others; sisters and friends pushing his manhood with provoking laughter and familiar jest. That night he proved himself.

They could not let him have the bride without a show of loud protest. On her return, they lay protectively round her and, in the darkness before the dawn, led her to Bomu's cattle byre to call for help. Pacing back and forth, leaning on a spear brought from her father's home, she uttered anguished cries of loneliness and fear, the requiem of girlhood. Behind her followed the weeping girls, aware that marriage was a beginning and an end.

The sun rose high, and in despair Sicenga cried,

> "Come rescue me, my kinsmen,
> Arm and let us go.
> The bird wanders.
> Bring me back, bring me back,
> Back to my home.
> Come and rescue me, my kinsmen."

The men of the bridal group had been hiding, awaiting this appeal, and out they rushed, Timba to the fore, striking their shields and shouting, "We come, Sister, we come, Sicenga."

They rushed the cattle byre and released the prisoners, fleeing with them to the veld. But the gesture, they knew, was in vain.

From Bomu's folk came the call, "We bring you back, Mother, with a cow, a white cow with red stripes. Return, our mother."

Sicenga halted, panting like a trapped deer, and to her came her mother-in-law-to-be, lips drawn in placating, toothless smile, eager for service from young unbroken girls. "Welcome, my child. Do not turn your back on this home, which recognizes virtue where it lies." With a show of gratitude, Sicenga's group accepted her new *rôle*.

Meekly, she presented gifts from her home to the in-laws who held her future happiness in their cleft tongues. With inscrutable eyes they watched her move towards the groom, holding in her open palm small beads, some red, some white. Which would he choose? With steady hand, the young chief picked a white. She was a virgin bride for all to see. Praise the ancestors. He bent his head, and over it she slipped with slightly trembling fingers a necklace of purity, which lay glistening on his dark, smooth chest. Now Bomu's folk wooed her with gifts, and brought her water, essence of life. Deliberately, vaunting reluctance still, she spilt the liquid, but they fetched her more. There was no escape. She gave libation to her husband's home.

Then came an old woman seamed with loose skin, superfluous now, but in her fertile days it lay in taut protection of her many pregnancies. Her old hands guided the novice to the cattle byre and she bade her sit with outstretched legs while a child, a little struggling babe, was laid upon her lap with words of hope: "Here is your child." The ancient hag then smeared the bride and babe with melting fat and red ochre, creating symbolic unity, the continuity of life.

At last Sicenga stood up and returned to her hut, where she sat silent and subdued amidst her girlhood friends. Late into the night they talked, and the fire grew grey and cold on the hearth and finally sleep came to Sicenga, a heavy, dreamless sleep. Beside her, Lamtana tossed and turned, restless, unsure, afraid. She could not always escape.

The next day they had to leave Sicenga. In Bomu's shrine hut, the senior men entrusted her to Bomu's home and ancestors. Farewells are always sad, but tears were not allowed, and she did not weep as she watched her friends depart. Then she went to the river to wash and prepare herself for the first night alone.

The village felt hollow without Sicenga, and the children seemed to quarrel amongst themselves more frequently than before. When Lamtana heard Totwa's young brother tease Sipiwo, "You aren't the child of a chief," she realized it was time to let him go to Feka's home. Three years is old enough to be separated from the mother, and it was following custom to let a child live in the home of grandparents. Had things been normal, she thought sadly, it would have been to her own parents that she would have sent her first son, but as it was, he needed to be sent from them.

Nabo Feka, who could not resist coming to see the child, though she was always received by Nabo Lamtana with undisguised hostility, could hardly believe her good fortune. And Sipiwo left his mother and her kin happily enough, excited by promises of bird snaring and hunting with Timba, the "little father."

The child had been gone only a couple of days when, early one morning, Lamtana saw Timba hastening to the village, and she rushed out to get his news. His face was tense, and without waiting to greet him she shouted at him, "What has happened to my child?"

He half-paused to reply, "The child is well, but the father of Feka is ill."

"Ill?"

"Yes. Very. I must hurry. He sent me to the chief. Take me to him."

"Wait and I'll tell him."

Mhau was being entertained by one of the younger wives and asked, "What is it?" a trifle impatiently at the interruption.

"There is someone with heavy news."

Her voice was so grave that, though he might have wished to say "Let him wait," he said, "Damn it, let him come here."

For once he missed Mpisi, but Mpisi was away at a cattle post for a few days, and now anyone could interrupt him.

Lamtana did not wait for Timba to finish with the chief, but went herself to Mputuya's home, with no idea of what she was going to do when she got there, but feeling impelled to go.

Mputuya was half-sitting, half-lying in the sand with a grey blanket drawn round his shoulders, and beside him was Sipiwo, his grandson, merrily beating an empty jam tin with a stick. At the child's joyous welcome, Mputuya raised his face. The girl stifled a cry of horror, then quickly turned down her eyes as custom demanded. But this was no customary situation, for which stereotyped phrases and gestures were ready provided. They had to handle it with a code forged from their own experiences of life.

"Sit, young bride." Timba's mother, who had hobbled out to

see who had arrived, brought her a mat, and she sat. The child climbed over her and she caressed him.

There was a silence. "Have you come to see the child or me?"

"I heard you were ill. I came." Her voice faltered.

"You see that I am sick. Will you stay? We have waited for you." Pause. "I am with cough. You and your children will give the homestead life."

She looked at him again, and this time was unable to tear her eyes from his face. The skin was crinkled and yellow like dried tobacco leaf, and the long jagged scar stood out dark and smoothly ugly. The ridges of the eye-sockets protruded like the lips of a clay bowl, and the balls of the big eyes were yellow and the pupils unnaturally bright. His hair, the colour of sheep's wool, was cropped close to the skull and gave the effect of a skeleton head.

She tried to speak, but her lips cracked and there was no voice in her throat. How could she refuse to come to his homestead and give it life? The familiar phrase "and a son shall bring a wife to waken the ashes of his father's home" became personally meaningful. But in the process, would she not turn herself to ashes? The child was patting her cheek for attention, and she put her arms round him and could say nothing.

Mputuya perceived her anguish. "Do you want to know how it happened?" His voice was impersonal; he was comforting her. He was prepared to rouse her to pity.

Pulling the blanket tightly round him, he stared past her to Goli, and began his story at the end.

"The white mine doctor thought he could cure me, but he saw only part of the truth. He didn't see that before the cough came I had already been killed. Killed by that person whom I have long sought, that person who is no husband to my sister and no father to his child."

Lamtana looked at Timba's mother and saw that she had her

hand over her face and tears were trickling between her bony fingers. The voice went on. "I found him drinking in a house in Sophiatown. The place was full of people and smoke and noise, and I had bought a drink that burnt my blood. And then I saw him staring at me and laughing, and I went up to him. He was smart, with a tie and a jacket, and when I came to him he drew back. I said, 'At last I have found you, you . . .' And I told him to take the sickness from off my sister. But he laughed at me and said, 'Who is your sister, that I should take a sickness off her?' And he spat in front of me, as though I were a dog." He breathed sharply in agitation and his voice could hardly support the load of its emotions. "And he pointed at me with his finger and cursed with a great curse, saying, 'Who will look after his women when he dies?' So he threw his witchcraft at me. Then, as he laughed again, I hit him with my stick with all my strength. He had no prophet's cap to save him. I killed him, sure. His body fell, soft as porridge." At this stage he began to cough so that his body seemed torn apart like two sides of a slaughtered beast. The women, listening to the rasping tear, could say nothing. He had to go on. "Before those in the house could stop me, I ran away. I knew what would happen if the police there caught me. They would not believe that he was the murderer, for they would only have seen him dead and me alive. They could not see you," and he looked pityingly at his sister. "Nor me as I am now."

Again he coughed, a dry, rattling cough, and again he continued. "Outside, it was raining and I ran and ran. I had come to the town by train, but I ran back more quickly by foot. I got to the mine and went on shift. When I came out from below, I knew his curse had found me. I was shaking like grass in the wind." His breath came in great gulps, and sweat shone on his forehead and above his wide upper lip. With tremendous effort he resumed his story. "I found an *nyanga* who doctored me. I did all he said. He wanted money. I gave him all I had. I even gave him my silver-headed stick. But it didn't help. Nothing helped. I couldn't sleep at night and began to cough. When the doctor examined us that month he sent me to hospital, where I stayed three weeks. But I refused to die there, and he let me out. He gave me papers for my sickness. I will die at home."

No one offered a word of hope or comfort, and the only sound came from Sipiwo, who, having lost interest in the grown-ups some time back, was again busy with his jam tin.

Again the cough. "Bring me water."

His hands shook so that he could not drink without spilling. Lamtana remembered Feka boasting that his father could flick off a fly from the back of an ox with a whip six feet long and carry a hut single-handed. He seemed to read her thoughts.

"Timba will work now, instead of me. Feka must go on learning." Her duty he left unsaid.

She felt trapped. He had aroused her pity, but the anguish she felt for herself was not lessened.

Timba returned while she was wondering miserably why she had come, and with him was the chief. She shrank back from her father, but Mhau looked only at his friend.

"Sorcerers have killed you." The words were forced from him.

"Yes. I am finished." But Mputuya's pleasure in seeing the chief was wonderful to behold; for one so great to come to a dying subject was indeed proof of deepest friendship. And he could not control himself in his weakness, but heaved out a great sob.

Lamtana, unable to bear any more, went away unnoticed, and without committing herself. But that they spoke of her when she had gone was clear from a remark made later by her mother. "I will never change my mind and let you go to that place of trouble." Lamtana was quite sure her mother was not acting entirely from affection, but was grateful all the same, and sympathized with her in her increasing isolation. For months the chief had not called her to him as a wife, and as the months passed she had grown more malicious and less beautiful.

Mputuya's sickness increased, and messages were sent to inform relatives, who came from far and near to enquire how he was getting on, showing by their sympathy that they were innocent of any evil wishes against him. Old Helemu, the generous and wise headman of the homestead on the road to Mbabane, was most solicitous, and Mputuya told him—as elder of his family council—as well as his wife, what wealth he had in cattle, and to whom he had loaned out certain beasts, and what cash he had and where it was hidden. In addition to his last wages he had fifteen pounds in cash, received in compensation for the sickness that, according to the doctor, was caught in the mine. It helped him to know that he was not leaving his family entirely impoverished, and that he had a careful wife and a trustworthy relative to see to the heavy expenses of death; there would not be very much left over after that.

His friend Potopoto made the long journey by bus, obtaining special leave from Lizulu, and he tried to make Mputuya feel at peace by telling him that he knew it would be easy for Feka to get a good post in the administration with all his qualifications. Mputuya said, "Let him go on learning. He has not yet got the white man's secrets." Only when he knew his days on earth were few would Mputuya let his wife send for Feka.

A terrible storm marked Feka's return. Lightning burnt the black clouds, thunder clapped the world, and rivers flowed from the sky. Feka's suit soaked into his body, and his shoes, which were quite new, and of which he was very proud, squelched with thick mud before he had a chance to take them off and carry them.

There were no trees under which he could shelter, and on reaching home he went straight to his hut and changed into Timba's spare trousers and khaki shirt. Afraid of death, he dreaded seeing his father and was glad of the delay and waited nervously for someone to tell his parents he had come.

The storm ended as suddenly as it had started. He went outside and saw his own child, his Sipiwo, jumping and splashing in a puddle. But the child did not recognize him and, when he called, "Sipiwo," looked a little startled and solemn. "Come here, my child."

He came slowly, pushing up the mud with his toes.

Feka bent his knees to be at his level and said, "You have grown. Tell your granny your father is here."

The child went obediently, without showing any emotion, but his granny came hurrying out and on seeing Feka took his hand and kissed it.

"How is he?"

"He is killed. Let us go to him."

Mputuya recognized his son and greeted him with a twisted smile. But Feka looked and could not smile. He sat with his head down like a woman. When Timba came in it was easier, and when Mputuya asked how he was getting on at school he was proud in his answer.

Mputuya listened and said, "Don't stay here after I have been buried. Push on with your learning," and Feka promised.

Mputuya died at sunset, the hour when ancestral spirits are closest to their earthly descendants. Lamtana, returning with Totwa from the gardens, heard the shrill keening and said bitterly, "They only cry for the dead."

Again messages were sent to the kinsmen, and those who could hurried to bid the dead a last farewell and to be strengthened against the contagion of death. Those who could not come sought protection from their own medicine men, for the newly dead are lonely and seek companionship from the living. The widow and the son, who were in particular danger, required the strongest protection, and in addition to the traditional specialists, Preacher Sikonyela, the priest of her church, the Holy Apostolic Church of Jesus in Zion, and members of the congregation, all dressed in white and singing hymns of glory, hastened to give comfort.

Preacher Sikonyela was a divine old man whose contact with God was direct, personal, and completely trusting. Between Sikonyela and old Helemu, who represented Mputuya's line, there was mutual tolerance; the Beginning was long ago, and there was only one Beginning.

Because Mputuya was not a convert, Helemu automatically took control, directing the mourners into correct demonstrations of grief but not interfering in any way with the singing and praying. Feka, heart-sore and dazed, did whatever he was told with mechanical relief. He did not want to think for himself, and the world of the white man's books seemed completely remote.

They killed a black ox to provide a shroud of hide, and the body looked curiously squat and unlike his father's with the knees bent up towards the chin in the position of a child in the womb. The widow insisted that they also send for a "box" from Simon. This had to be made, and it delayed the burial so that the smell of death seemed to stifle the living, and fat black-green flies settled everywhere.

Day and night his closest and dearest held vigil. At night the autumn wind howled, trying to force an entry through the reed fence.

In her hut far away, Lamtana lay thinking, "Feka is back. What shall I do? Who can help me? I love my child and I want his father. But I am me, and I will have to live with the old women and be their slave. My life will dry up like earth without rain. I will have no more thoughts to write on paper. No, I cannot go to him. I will not go to him."

The wind was screeching through the reeds like an owl of ill omen. She shut her eyes and tried to imagine herself the Lady of the Lamp, but instead there appeared the suffering face of Mputuya. Her hard, short nails clawed into her palms to stop her from screaming and waking her companions. Would daylight never come?

At dawn, with Feka holding the head and Helemu the feet, six men carried Mputuya to the big shallow grave dug, in the shape of a hut and a yard, at the entrance of his cattle byre.

They rested the box for a while before lowering it into the earth, and they lifted the lid for the mourners to look on the face for the last time.

Timba's mother flung herself forward, shrieking hysterically, "Bury me with him. My brother. Take me, too." Helemu pushed her back firmly and said brutally, "It is not your grave." And Timba looked at her with pity while she wept, a little apart from the widow, who was surrounded by her relatives and the congregation of her church.

Sikonyela led the hymns for the dead.

> "Tears are wiped away,
> All pain is past.
> Would that we were with them,
> With those holy people.
> Praise the Lord,
> Saviour of the dead,
> Jesus, our King."

Carefully the six set the dead in his new home, and Feka threw down the first sod, which thumped on the wooden box. The praying stopped as the women mourners wept without restraint and the kinsmen covered the grave with the earth from the byre. They brought in his cattle to trample down the mound, and to Feka it seemed wrong that his father should be dead and his cattle living. It was right that some of the best be killed for the dead.

All those kin who had been weakened by touching the corpse were purified, and those who were closest to him were fortified again for life. The shaven head, the limbs marked with little streaks of doctored blood, the bitter-tasting medicines—these were comforts defined by custom, but they did not fill the emptiness or stifle the fears.

Feka remained at home for one week, and then reluctantly went back to school; his head was shaven and on his sleeve his mother sewed a broad black band. Not once had he spoken to, or even seen, Lamtana, and he could not understand how in his sadness she could avoid him and their son. He had held the child in his arms while Hlubi, the medicine man, scraped the hair off his little round head and made the incisions necessary for safety on the firm little body, and the child had screamed all the time with hatred and fear.

Lamtana had not even come with the women of Mhau's home, on their visit to the widow. Though Nabo Sicenga and Nabo Totwa had argued that because of Lamtana's ties through Sipiwo, first grandson of the deceased, she should be specially purified, her mother had replied that her daughter was not Feka's wife and should not appear so in a public ritual. She bought from Hlubi a special medicine for Lamtana to chew in solitude so that the dead would not think of her in anger and torment her in dreams.

The widow and Nabo Timba sat secluded in their hut of death, weeping and lamenting their loss. Sympathizers, on coming within shouting distance of the hut of death, would begin to wail or pray and those inside would respond accordingly. And some who, like Mpisi and Nabo Lamtana, were not really sad that Mputuya was dead, could always weep loudly in recollection of their own miseries, and the truly bereaved noticed the tears but did not know for whom they fell.

In the winter of the following year, when Feka came home for his holidays, the family gave final offerings to Mputuya's spirit, that it might stay quietly in the old home. Thereafter Timba was free to seek work in the city to pay for Feka's schooling.

Old Helemu asked Feka's mother if she would like to move near to his own homestead, but she refused. Too old to be taken as wife, she was also too independent to seek constant protection from her dead husband's kin. Besides, the old place had memories. She would move the huts no farther than was necessary, and cultivate the old site made fertile with dung from the cattle byre and marked by the grave of Mputuya, the headman. Helemu respected her decision and suggested, without being asked, that he send one of his own several sons, a lad of twelve or thirteen, whose mother was dead, to live with her and help when Timba left. Everyone was pleased, knowing it was good for children to be with kin away from home as long as they were well cared for.

The grandchild, Sipiwo, continued to be quite happy without his mother, whom he saw only occasionally. Timba was his favourite "father," and far more dear to him than Feka, who came each time as a stranger bringing gifts from Goli.

When Sipiwo heard that Timba was going to Goli to work, he felt Feka was responsible and attacked him with fury, shouting, "Go away, you. Leave him." Then, rushing into the hut where he had put a shiny cigarette tin, the most precious of his gifts, he flung it at Feka, screaming, "Take that instead."

At that moment, there was a striking resemblance between Sipiwo and his absent mother. Timba was the first to rebuke the child, but the incident deeply angered Feka's mother, who was less sorry than she might otherwise have been at Timba's approaching departure. Of Timba's own mother's feelings there was no sign. To let her son go was her last service to the brother who had cared for her and been killed on her account; it was right that Timba should work to help Feka continue at school.

Both boys went with others of Mhau's subjects to pay tax for the first time. Without a tax receipt Timba knew he could not get a man's pay, and Feka was required to carry a scholar's-exemption pass. Mhau was not present. He had sent a message with Mpisi, whose tax was paid by him, to explain that he was not well but would make an effort to come along later.

Mpisi greeted the boys with bluff heartiness. "Now you, too, are men."

"Indeed, Father," replied Timba politely, but Feka pretended not to hear, thinking, "Why should I agree with this man who should have done what my father did—and been dead in his place?"

The administration police had put up a large square tent, and Mr. Tootles, whose duties included tax collecting, was in charge of the business side. He was assisted on the clerical and vocal side by the policeman-interpreter, whose conspicuously gesticulating arm sported an additional stripe on its smart khaki drill. As the morning's work had not yet begun, the new sergeant was holding forth on the advantages of a tent, rain-proof, easily portable, and "sifilized." This word, alien to the uneducated Swazi, interested Feka, who, partly to show off his learning, corrected him politely. "I think you mean 'civilized,' not 'sifilized.' "

With scorn the interpreter replied, "Never. Civilized is what those people are," and he waved his decorated arm over the assortment of taxpayers; "sifilized is what we are," and he graciously included the tent with Mr. Tootles in his sweep.

Feka was prepared to argue the point, but the hour of nine was about to strike and Mr. Tootles called impatiently, "Sergeant."

"Sir." Arms and heels clicked smartly to attention.

"Bring the registers."

These were produced and laid with a flourish on a table in the entrance. Mr. Tootles, sitting on a canvas chair, read out the names, which the sergeant relayed as effectively as any loudspeaker for the benefit of the crowd collected on the veld. The owner of the name came forward briskly enough if he had the money, reluctantly if he was without, and he would wait patiently while Tootles put down his pen, shook his pale head, inspected him through innocent, wide-open eyes, and reprimanded him.

"Another defaulter."

He was then informed that if he didn't pay by a specified time he would be imprisoned. "But," Tootles conceded, "workers are always needed on the farms and on the mines." Occasionally he added in a voice of suffering, "Ask those people how they think Government can provide schools and roads and other amenities if they don't pay tax." The interpreter neither expected nor received a reply.

Often a name was called and no one answered, and Mr. Tootles would say, "Uh?" expectantly, and bite the end of his pen while Mpisi would inform the interpreter that the person was working away from home, or ill, or too old, or dead.

"Too many people are ill or too old or dead today," Tootles complained petulantly. "They must get doctor's certificates if they don't come."

Old Beta grumbled, "It's ten years since I last paid tax, and each year I have to waste my legs to show I still have no teeth."

"Mputuya Zwane." The name boomed suddenly through the crowd. There was a silence, and Mpisi said in a troubled and angry voice, "It is a year since he went, but is his name still in the books?"

"He is dead," reported the interpreter.

Mputuya Zwane. It sounded familiar. Tootles suddenly remembered. That big, crazy guy who assaulted the prophet. Dead. He put his pen firmly through the name.

Twelve forty-five. Mr. Tootles disappeared inside the tent, the flap closed.

At two o'clock he reappeared, washed and brushed and ready to work again till four thirty sharp. Time already!

"Tell the rest of the men to come back tomorrow, early. And tell the chief I want to see him here as well."

Walking home, Timba asked, "What do the whites really do with all our money?"

A plump lout replied promptly, "They eat it. They can't live a day without money. They buy every mouthful."

This was very funny and everybody laughed, but Timba persisted, "Does our tax help us? Is it true to say that it gives us schools and roads and other things? Or are these just lies of the white man?"

To this Lubelo answered craftily, "Yes. They are deceiving

us. Missionaries pay for the schools, and the roads are made by white men for their cars. They know what they want our money for."

"I see. We ourselves get nothing from it?"

A brightly smiling lad called out, "Oh yes, we do. We go to jail."

All of them roared with laughter at the joke.

The new taxpayers were registered late the next afternoon. Feka produced a note from school, which Mr. Tootles carefully read and finally sanctioned. He wrote down Feka's name, excused him from paying, and gave him the necessary pass.

Timba went next. Looking at him, Mr. Tootles saw a lean, overgrown youth, his hair in the latest style of the young bachelors.

"Yes, it's time you paid your tax instead of idling away your time with the girls."

The crowd greeted this sally with delight—Timba was a recognized young blood. He himself accepted it as a compliment, and as he approached his friends he lifted his warrior's stick and shield and leapt like a deer in the air, chanting, "Hit the buck, strong arms. *Dji a oh.*"

His age-mates took up the refrain, a few of the men watched with approval, but old Beta commented, "Those are just children," and he jabbed viciously at his nostril with a long-nailed forefinger. "Before, men went to real war; now they fight rocks and papers. The earth is rotten."

A few of the lads decided to go together to earn their tax money. They did not even consider going to the farms; the mines were the recognized battle-fields. Timba recalled to himself how, a few days before Mputuya had died, he, Timba, had sat with him in the smoky darkness of the hut and Mputuya had once again told him that soon it would be necessary for him to go to work. He had tried to ask Mputuya what to expect, and Mputuya had dropped his bulging lids over his fever-bright eyes and spoken challengingly. "What it is like I can never tell you. A man can only see for himself." Well, he, Timba, would now see for himself.

He went with his pals to the Recruiting Office of the Chamber of Mines, near the court-house, and a couple of the defaulters were also there. They had been to the mines before and followed the routine without interest or any display of emotion, but the youths talked boastfully and laughed a lot.

They swaggered into the office, where a smart, mature clerk with the letters N.R.C. (Native Recruiting Corporation) on his shirt read out in a rapid monotone the contents of a long sheet of paper, and each recruit in turn was told to put an X in understandng. Glancing at the paper, Timba deciphered separate letters, e-m-p-l-o-y-, but the word itself was strange and he gave up the exercise with a comic blowing out of empty air. He knew more or less what the paper meant, no matter what it said. He was to work in a mine and earn money; the work was hard and dangerous, and the white man would not let him stop when he wanted, but when his time was up. Still, he would see the city and come back fledged as a warrior from the outside world.

He received a bus and a train ticket, and one pound and ten shillings, half his month's wages, in cash in advance.

When he came home he presented the money to Feka's mother, who gave back five shillings for his own requirements. Very proud of his first earnings, he waited for Feka, who had gone out without saying where he was going or when he would return, to accompany him to Simon's. In the meantime, he helped Sipiwo model an ox out of clay, and promised him sweets from the shop. Feka, who came in a little later, willingly agreed to go to Simon's. He volunteered no explanation for his absence and no one asked where he had been; he was the headman now.

The shop was full. Mr. Simon, who had already heard who had been recruited, greeted the boys and said to Timba, "So, my boy. You're going to the Golden City, too. What do you want? A trunk? A shirt? A bag of corn? It's a pity I didn't recruit you myself. Some traders have all the luck. Thirty shillings for every man they catch. Why the N.R.C. had to set up its own office here beats me. It's all the fault of this ——— government. It shouldn't let outsiders take the bread out of the mouths of its own settlers. We're the real backbone of the people. Where would they be without us? But we could starve for all they care." And so he rambled on, while the boys made occasional courteous interjections and examined the goods. Finally Timba bought a mouth-organ for two shillings, a bag of sweets for sixpence, and bread for one shilling; the remaining one shilling and sixpence he wrapped in a piece of old cloth to take with him to Goli.

On their way back Timba suggested, a little hesitantly, that they might pass Mhau's, but Feka said abruptly, "They aren't at home."

"Where did you see them?"

"At the gardens."

"Both?" The boys understood each other.

"Yes. Totwa, too. I was looking for Lamtana," he blurted out. "She does not look at me these days."

"Her father should have forced her to come to our home at the beginning," Timba suggested.

"It would not have helped. She is as obstinate as a stone. I cannot find out what it is she now hates in me," he said quite gloomily, and then added savagely, "Take care you, too, do not open the cattle kraal of the chief."

"Never," laughed Timba. "I will look after myself. I just wanted to show her I had joined. Her lover has never been farther than those mountains there."

A group of girls were coming towards them and Timba apparently forgot about Totwa and sauntered to meet them, losing little time in announcing that he had been recruited.

"*Hau! Hau!* The mine is fearful," said one of them, a handsome wench with bold, admiring eyes.

"It is war," he answered, and he felt a thrill of joy, or was it fear?

A few days later he left the green pastures of his home for the pits and shafts of the mine, and became another insignificant private in the great army of the industrial revolution of South Africa. And Feka returned, without solving his trouble, to his books in the school in Goli.

To the rhythmic *suf-suf* of soft grain rolled between rounded grinding stones, Nabo Sicenga hummed the lullaby with which she had rocked her children, and Nabo Totwa said affectionately as she recognized the song, "Soon Sicenga will be home with her marriage cattle and we'll hear her news."

"Yes. I only hope her in-laws treat her well."

"Do you know how many cattle will be sent with her?" came from Nabo Lamtana.

"No."

"Don't agree to less than fifteen. After all, her father is no commoner."

Nabo Sicenga bridled at the indirect jibe and said wryly, "I'll see that the cattle are enough."

A child ran in excitedly. "We've seen her. She's coming ahead of the men with the cattle, who are waiting on the road."

"How many?"

"We counted twenty."

"Twenty! They will want another girl as well," Nabo Lamtana exclaimed.

Totwa went out to meet Sicenga and brought her into the hut, exclaiming joyously, "Look how the bushveld loves her."

Everyone praised her. "How she shines."

"How plump she has grown."

And Nabo Sicenga repeated over and over again, "It is good to see you, my child."

Lamtana wished she could make inarticulate clicks of pleasure and show her feelings as obviously as the others. Picking up one of the small children, she caressed it so passionately that it yelled, whereupon the mother, one of Mhau's *umcwasho* wives, grabbed it from her.

From the entrance of the village, Bomu's men called, "We come with twenty cattle," and the last act of Sicenga's marriage contract began; a contract that gave her to the groom and his family forever, even beyond the death of either bride or groom. To show how deeply prized she was, her people had to drive off the bringers of mere cattle with sticks and blows, and the children rushed about shouting, "It's a fight. A real fight." The animals, blundering around in confusion, increased the shindy with loud, protesting bellows.

No one really considered twenty head too few, and when the mock resistance weakened, the besiegers drove their cattle into the byre of the chief. Mpisi officiously conducted the older members to quarters specially put aside for them, and the younger men went around in aggressive good humour, finally running off with a huge jurum of beer. The girls, led by Totwa, joined them in their hut, and there was drinking and ribald joke, and the girls pleased the men. Only Sicenga stayed with the mothers, who plied her with questions, and Lamtana came and stayed beside her.

Mhau, accompanied by Beta, went to welcome the men and discuss the final settlement. He stressed the worthiness of the girl, and the solicitude of her family for her well-being. Bomu's spokesman, a middle-aged man with a face nobly carved from old oak, appreciated the father's pride and fears, and promised that the girl would be respected and properly cared for. Of course, and he paused, it would be for her happiness to have a young sister as junior co-wife, and the cattle he had brought included some specifically for that purpose. Bomu trusted that Sicenga would not be the only daughter of the chief to rejoice him.

Beta pronounced approval. "It is good for two sisters to go to one man. It is custom."

Mhau agreed, and since a junior co-wife was less important than an independent senior wife, he felt he had no need to worry which particular sister would be considered suitable; the choice would be left mainly to Nabo Sicenga, who would, of course, consult him. Probably she would choose her own younger daughter, Velapi, conceived the night of the sale of beer for the first school uniforms; anyway, he was glad of a double tie with Bomu, who seemed a truly admirable son-in-law.

To seal the contract between their families, each side was required to provide a beast to be killed and shared equally between them. Mhau instructed Mpisi to point out the large black-and-white ox, which he and Beta had previously agreed upon, for the visitors to kill first.

The men placed themselves in strategic positions in the cattle byre. In her mother's hut, Sicenga was told to sit and grip with both hands the supporting pole of the hut, relinquishing it only when the sacrificial ox gave its last loud death cry. So would she peg down her place in the husband's home.

**177**

But something was wrong. When the ox was stabbed, it uttered no long, deep bellows to signify ancestral pleasure and acceptance of the offering. From the great soft jaws came only a short, half-stifled groan. Then followed an eerie silence, broken suddenly by piercing snorts from the herd, unnerved by the smell of blood. Sicenga dropped her hands quickly, and those with her shuddered in the sudden darkness of fear.

Outside the men gathered round the beast, speculating on what its silent death might mean. None of them could remember such a quick, ominously soundless, kill. Were the ancestors angered? If so, whose was the fault? A strange tension divided the two groups. They did not look at each other, but stared at the scarlet stream trickling from the neat wound onto the ground. Then Mhau turned to the men harshly. "Don't waste the blood," he ordered and walked off. He called his family council quickly in consultation. Could they continue with the ritual?

Old Beta judged, "The girl is clearly happy, and we know that her husband is all right. If his men agree, let us go on and finish."

Mhau sent for Bomu's men and put the question. "After what has happened, are you prepared to let your beast be killed?"

They, too, had reached a favourable conclusion, and their leader replied, "We have agreed. Let us go ahead. I am Bomu's mouth and he sent me to marry your daughter for him."

Mhau took a big pinch of snuff, offered some to his guests, and, sneezing with relief, congratulated them. "Bomu knows how to choose good men to serve him." He turned to Mpisi and ordered, "Kill the beast now," and the men returned to the cattle byre.

Mpisi felt the sharp point of the spear with his fingers, and went to perform the one task in which he had never yet failed. He led the way, whistling encouragingly and soothingly to the still tense herds. In one corner Bomu's herdsmen were keeping guard over the dead beast. Mpisi's assistants drove the animals towards the fence as he edged in and out, his taut, muscular body pressing lightly against their flanks, making space for himself. He felt quite sure of himself. His face was without its usual servility. Moving with a hunter's speed, he edged nearer to his prey. Once in striking range, he noted the exact spot into which to plunge his spear. Moving lightly forward, he raised his weapon. Down went the shiny blade. Deep between the ribs. There followed a loud, long bellow, then another and yet another. A gigantic chorus of supplication rolled through to the ancestors. As the herd crowded around, Mpisi slithered back into safety and servility.

The dying beast, its big dark eyes slowly glazing, lurched onto its knees, where it remained, uttering long groans, warming the hearts of the people, driving out the horror of the last, silent, slaughter, till, with a grotesque, almost human cry, it collapsed and rolled onto its side.

The men caught the blood in dishes, beat the skin from the carcass with huge flails, and hacked down the midriff. They took care not to break the membrane of the gall bladder, which would be bound round the arm of the girl selected as Sicenga's junior co-wife.

The mothers and sisters sat with Sicenga, waiting. Lamtana was on the outside of the group, perturbed by all she had seen and could not accept. She was secure only in the knowledge that on this occasion she would not be chosen for Bomu. Not for her the role of subordinate co-wife to a sister. She pushed out her lower lip, an odd but not unattractive habit she had acquired when concentrating. Her wide, beautiful eyes searched the faces of the girls around her; they were content. Why was she so restless, seeking a future so different from past and present? She looked at the mothers, and her stomach turned over quickly as she realized the isolation of her own mother from her co-wives. "Yes," she thought. "It is true. Almost everything comes from the mother who bears one, and suckles one, and trains one. They say that witchcraft goes from a mother to her child; no man can pass on that power."

Her thoughts were interrupted by a sudden thump, as a youngster from Bomu's group flung in through the doorway the full gall bladder, precious symbol of a gift supplicated and received. Almost before it fell and burst, Velapi, who had grown into a nimble-footed copy of slim Sicenga, picked it up and rushed with it back to the hut of Bomu's men and threw it in. The gall leaked along the way, leaving a symbolic patch. The messenger quickly picked it up and ran back to Sicenga's hut, pursued by Velapi. So the race went on till both runners were exhausted, the bitter liquid was all spilt, and the thick, empty membrane remained with Sicenga's group.

The laughter and excitement died down. Slowly and solemnly Nabo Sicenga blew her breath into the membrane and bound the long oval balloon round the arm of Velapi as Sicenga's younger sister.

The child was pleased and proud, and, watching her, Lamtana knew that if all went well, she would grow up happy in the knowledge that when mature enough she would go as a little wife to the good Bomu, where her own sister Sicenga, whom she loved dearly, would welcome her. It was a future not to be despised. Yet she, Lamtana, despised it. The cheerful, friendly voice of Totwa was calling her to feast.

It was wonderful to have Sicenga back. She had permission from Bomu to stay a whole moon, and for a few days all was merry-making.

Then something happened, something so terrible that no one who was present can ever forget it. It haunts their waking hours and makes them cry out loud in their sleep.

The day had been very peaceful. The women and girls had come together to Nabo Sicenga's yard to scrape the dried corn from the cobs for storing in the underground granaries. The work needed patience and strong hands, but was not strenuous.

The hard yellow and white grains steadily piled like thousands of big strong teeth on the ground, and the cobs, excellent for burning, were thrown into high heaps. Sicenga was helping her mother. Nabo Lamtana was less vicious than usual, and there was a general air of relaxation and harmony. Later, Lamtana would remember it as an uneventful, routine day in late winter.

That night Sicenga complained of a headache. No one took much notice, but in the middle of the night Lamtana felt her tossing restlessly.

"What is it?" she asked sleepily.

"My head is killing me."

Her teeth chattered so that she could hardly speak, yet when Lamtana felt her body it was burning. Alarmed, Lamtana lit the candle and sat up. Sicenga's eyes were glazed, and her neck jerked and twitched on the hard wooden pillow. Quickly Lamtana got up and, wrapping a blanket round her, hastened to Nabo Sicenga's hut.

She knocked vigorously, gasping, "Mother, Sicenga is sick."

The words reached the mother as part of a bad dream, which she tried to shake from her till she realized with horror that it was no dream. Stumbling to her feet still half-asleep, she blundered to the hut where her daughter was lying. She gave one look at the girl and screamed, "The witches. What have they done?"

In every illness there lurks a germ of fear, more malignant, more potent, more frequently fatal than any other germ. Sometimes it is dormant, but given the slightest encouragement it multiplies, procreating and feeding on itself. So it was with the sickness of Sicenga.

Quickly the news spread, and a multiplicity of fears clouded the minds of the villagers. The chief dispatched a messenger on foot to Bomu to inform him that his wife was ill. At the same time he sent for Hlubi, the medicine man.

"Is it fever alone?" asked the father anxiously.

Hlubi turned his wizened face to Mhau, but his squint

seemed to look inward on itself. "Perhaps it is fever, perhaps it is something else. We will see."

He did not seem to bother about the patient. Squatting on the ground, he undid the calabashes and pouches tied round his person. From one of the pouches he took his divining bones, shook them in cupped hands, and threw them on the floor. He bit a piece of root and spat on the bones and called on his forefathers for help. Then, with slow deliberate movements, he began his diagnosis. "Here is the child, this is a river, here are those of her home that have come too close to her. They are drawing in on her. That is bad. Here is her husband, here is her husband's family. The river separates her. Here is her father, pushed away."

He gathered up the bones and repeated the performance, and this time he scarcely spoke as he pushed his long finger over the ground gently, moving the main pieces. When he had finished, he muttered as though to himself, "It is bad. There is something the matter in this village."

"Will she be saved?" Nabo Sicenga burst out, her face distorted by grief and anxiety. "Can you save my child?"

He looked at her and past her. "Quiet, woman, I have work to do."

With him was his assistant-apprentice—a pale-faced boy with white beads in his hair. Soon the two were busy grinding up herbs, which they put in a potsherd on the hearth. For the first time, the *nyanga* approached the patient and with a rusty blade made small cuts on her forehead and on her joints, and into the cuts he rubbed the charred medicines.

When he had finished, he went to Mhau. "I will return tomorrow; I want a goat, to finish the treatment."

"How is she?" begged the father.

"I am not yet sure; I think she will be well."

They moved Sicenga to her mother's hut and all that night Nabo Sicenga sat by her daughter's side, her eyes bloodshot from lack of sleep and suppressed tears, her serenity seared by suspicions. Nabo Totwa had brought in special food, and stayed with her for a long while trying to show the depth of her sympathy and love. But the dainty dishes were left untasted and Nabo Sicenga did not chase away the flies that gathered on the bowl's rim, and when all Nabo Totwa's words—and for once she had struggled for words—failed to awaken any response, she left, yawning wearily.

Nabo Lamtana had also made an attempt to cross the mother's barrier of fear and grief, and had sent in a little pot of beer. She did not go in herself; she knew that she could never make the other understand that she had a morbid dread of sickness, and she could not bear the thought of watching Sicenga's suffering. The beer she sent was left untouched; the absence of the sender was noticed.

Hlubi returned early the next morning and Mpisi brought him the goat required for the treatment. The assistant slaughtered the animal, cutting its throat and catching its blood in a broken calabash. The master specialist worked without haste, snipping off little bits from here and there and giving orders. He burned the pieces of flesh, added herbs, and poured on the blood, so that a thick smoke exuded through the yard. Then he told his assistant to cut reeds and hollow them, and ordered Nabo Sicenga to fetch her daughter and the other girls of her age.

Sicenga was so weak she could hardly sit up when they brought her into the sunlight, and Lamtana and Totwa supported her on either side. Hlubi told his assistant to give each girl a reed and commanded them, "Inhale." Putting one end of the reed into the thick smoke and the other into her mouth, each girl inhaled; the fumes choked them, making them splutter, filling their lungs so that they coughed painfully and tears poured down their cheeks. Hlubi would not let them stop until the last of the smoke had died away. Sweat was pouring from them. They dragged Sicenga back in to the hut.

"It is more than fever," Hlubi said to Mhau. "It will need all my strength to cure, and the help of your ancestors as well. I will return tomorrow."

As the sun set, Mhau went into the cattle byre, and, standing in the midst of his herds with his eyes to the east, he addressed the dead. "You, my father, what are you saying about this? Is she not your child as well as mine? What have I done that you should destroy my home? Why are you killing me? Do I not give you food? Are these not your animals? Let her live, my fathers. Let her name be widespread. She is my oldest child. Help her. She is without sin." His words rang out in the stillness. In their huts the women and children listened quietly, with heavy hearts.

The next morning Sicenga was worse. When Hlubi came he said, "She is possessed. They have put wild animals into her. They must be made to come out."

He gave her a potion of crushed bulbs and wild plants and the black seed of the *datura*.

A sudden frenzy seized the sick girl. She writhed and twisted and shouted words that no one could understand. Her breath came in sharp hisses as she tried to drag herself along the floor. The specialist looked on. "Didn't I tell you?" His voice was almost triumphant. "Didn't I tell you that wild animals have been put into her?" Suddenly he shot at her in a voice of command, "Speak, tell us what you are, come out, speak." But the noises continued to be incomprehensible, and suddenly Sicenga collapsed and white foam trickled from her mouth.

"She is very ill. The witches refuse to give her up."

When Lamtana and Totwa went to find out how she was, they found the mother crouched behind her on the floor of the hut and the doctor still busy with medicines in a corner. The two girls hesitated in the doorway.

"Who is there?" asked Nabo Sicenga mechanically.

"We. Totwa and Lamtana," Totwa answered, since Lamtana said nothing.

"Come in."

The hut was hot and smoky from the fire on the hearth. Sicenga was lying as near to the fire as possible, and little flames lit up her face as the two girls looked at her. She made no sign of recognition.

"My sister, how are you? Speak," Totwa pleaded, trying to restrain her tears.

Lamtana, shocked and distressed beyond words, could not utter a sound. Suddenly she became conscious that Nabo Sicenga's swollen eyes were fixed on her with bleak hostility. She turned away her head and stared again at the sick girl's face. Only a few days ago everyone had said, "How she shines," and now there was no lustre, almost no life. Incisions made by the doctor on her forehead and throat had drawn blood that lay clotted in thin dark streaks. Lamtana found herself hypnotized by the blood, and it seemed to her that Sicenga's life was drying up in it. The soft features grew blurred as Lamtana looked.

Nabo Sicenga broke the silence with a low, spoken wail. "This that has happened is beyond my strength. The bad resist the wizards, while the good are overcome."

Lamtana tried to speak and instead burst out weeping loudly. There was a momentary shock of silence, then the mother shouted in frenzy, "Stop that noise! Is she dead already, that you weep thus? Get out."

Lamtana stumbled out, trying to choke back her sobs.

Totwa followed her and said with suppressed fury, "How could you do that? Don't you know that loud weeping is forbidden until the person is dead?"

Lamtana had no excuse. She did not even try to offer one.

No word had come from Bomu; the messenger travelling on foot could only have reached his village that morning, and he would have no idea how seriously the illness had developed. Deeply conscious of his responsibility to the in-laws, Mhau sent Mpisi to Simon to ask him to telephone for him to the commissioner's office at Stegi, the office nearest to Bomu's home, and ask someone there to give him the latest bulletin.

That same afternoon the reply came back. The husband said, "Take her at once to the hospital in Mbabane."

Mhau was shocked, and Beta at first refused even to consider the suggestion. But they realized that, by accepting the final sacrificial animal, her family had handed over control to Bomu and his kin and could not by tribal law refuse their explicit request. They called Nabo Sicenga.

At first she wept, "This is no white man's sickness." But when Hlubi shuddered and said, "The witches are overcoming me," she voiced the deepest of all fears. "Perhaps she will be safer in the white man's hospital than in this home." No one missed the undertone of bitter suspicion and indirect accusation.

So the chief finally sent Mpisi to Simon to beg him to drive the girl up in his car, which had on more than one occasion helped the local folk in emergencies.

Since the death of his beloved Lomusa, Simon had avoided taking people to the government hospital at Mbabane and preferred driving them the extra distance to one of the bigger mission hospitals. But Mpisi made it clear that Bomu had stated Mbabane specifically, and Simon, out of friendship to Mhau, felt obliged to agree. But he could not face the memory of another journey there by night. He sent a message back that his car had no lights; he was prepared to take her early tomorrow. Tomorrow was accepted as soon enough.

It was decided that someone from the home go with her, to keep her company in the ward and send reports back to her family. How dearly Lamtana wished that she could go and serve Sicenga, but she dared not even suggest it. For this task, a reliable elderly woman, not even a mother, was considered the most suitable attendant, and Mhau selected Mpisi's wife.

Simon arrived quite early in his car, an old Chevrolet, which had seen better days and better driving. Undaunted by the fact that the chief's home was almost a mile from the main road,

Simon bumped along over the foot-path across the veld, and Mrs. Simon bumped beside him.

She was wearing her best dress, a pretty dress of floral nylon over a pink slip, and on her head was a small pink straw hat with a bunch of daisies at the side.

"You're not going to a wedding," Simon had said irritably. "Why are you all dressed up?"

"If you don't like it, I'll stay at home. I'm only going because you asked me, not because I want to."

"Oh, come on. I'll need your help."

Normally she did not go with him to Mbabane; he always stopped in at the pub for a drink, or two or three, and then if he came out with a drinking companion and found her waiting for him he would introduce her in a loud voice as "my house-keeper," in English. She could not face the looks of mingled interest, curiosity, and disdain that this obvious evasion usually aroused. But this time he had told her that she must come to help with the girl. He was never at ease with sick women; they made him too unhappy.

The chief came out to thank Simon and instruct him to give full details to the doctor and get his report, all of which Simon promised to do.

Sicenga, wrapped in a blanket, was half-carried by her mother and Mpisi's wife to the back of the car. When Mpisi's wife had scrambled in beside her, the mother brought little parcels of uncooked sweet potatoes and monkey nuts for her to prepare for the girl. She had heard that hospital food was never tasty.

Lamtana came to speak to Mrs. Simon, but the younger children were there, clamouring for sweets and examining the car, separating her from her friend.

Simon beckoned her nearer and asked loudly in English, "Why not come with us? You could help at the hospital."

Nabo Sicenga thrust her head into his window. "What are you saying to her? Why are you speaking to her in English? We are Swazi and she is also a Swazi. Speak so that we can all understand. What did you say?"

Taken aback by the violence of emotion in the woman's face and voice, Simon repeated his request in Swazi.

At this the gentle Nabo Sicenga lost all self-control.

"Why do you want *her* to go with? Why choose that one? I am sending away my daughter to save her life. Are you wanting her to die? Oh, my fathers," she wailed. "The witches are too strong."

Nabo Totwa pulled her back. "It is bad to speak like that. Be quiet, now. Simon is just a fool.Come. Let them go."

Mhau intervened harshly. "Shut up. Your daughter is going with Mpisi's wife and Simon's wife. Nabo Totwa, take her to her hut to rest. Start the car, Simon."

"O.K., Chief." He leered at Lamtana. "Seems you're not coming."

The car lurched forward. The children screeched and scattered. Mpisi's wife poked her head out of the window and waved vigorously. The children waved back; a few chased after the car. Nabo Totwa led away the weeping Nabo Sicenga. Mhau and Mpisi walked off together. Nabo Lamtana was not present. She was busy grinding the corn from the cobs.

Lamtana stood alone. "What has happened?" she wondered. Her head whirled. "I am a stone. I can't move. I can't cry. Why did Simon speak to me in English? Why did he have to ask me to go with her? How am I different? What have I done? Sicenga, my sister, I wanted to help you. I have done nothing to you." Her voice came back. She screamed loudly, "I have done nothing. Nothing." She ran after the car, and the dust that lay heavy in the still air choked her cries. She fell down in the arid road and wept.

Mpisi's wife, peering through the back window, commented, "She wanted to come, but they were right to refuse."

Mrs. Simon said scathingly to her husband, "You know you

should have asked her father. How can a girl go without permission?"

He drove erratically, just missing a few cattle that strayed casually across his path. Twice he hit enormous potholes that threw his passengers up to the roof.

"Hang on to her," he yelled to Mrs. Simon. "This damn road. Why can't they fix it?" And every now and then he shouted, "Is she still alive?"

In less than three hours they could see the houses of Mbabane. Simon raced rattling down the last long, winding hill marked "Danger," nearly colliding with a large railway bus churning round a bend. He dashed along the main road of the town and drew up with a loud scream of brakes outside the long white hospital building.

Leaving the women in the car, Simon walked up the steps, to be met by the matron. She, like everyone else, had heard the arrival of his car and stepped outside to make an inspection. Having satisfied her curiosity with one searching stare, she asked, with the scantiest of preliminary courtesies, "What have you brought?" She looked, and smelt, so specklessly clean and antiseptic after the dust and sickness in the car that Simon felt himself stammering like a gangling boy, "I've brought a sick woman, ma'am. Chief Mhau's eldest daughter."

"Can she walk by herself?"

"Hardly, ma'am. She's not moved since we got her into the car. We—"

She cut him short. "I will send an orderly to bring her in. Please come with me and give me some particulars."

The thud of his boots on the shiny floor sounded to him like the pounding of his heart. To this same place he had brought Lomusa. He could hardly answer the routine questions and wanted only to get away. Through the pain of memory he heard the cool English voice say that the doctor was operating at the moment; if Mr. Simon liked, he could wait or come back in half an hour.

"I'll come back," he gulped, and headed for the car.

Mrs. Simon and Mpisi's wife helped the orderly bring Sicenga inside. Mrs. Simon returned alone and climbed into the front seat beside Simon. As they drove off, she saw the matron's washed-out eyes follow them through the office window. Their expression was utterly contemptuous. Mrs. Simon winced. She looked at Simon. A big loose man with a purple network on his thick nose, dirty, broken teeth, a crumpled shirt without a tie, and inside this exterior a great emptiness that *she* had never filled. Gladys Simon drew into her corner, as far away from him as the closed door allowed. Yes. She was contemptible. Not because she was black and he was white. But because he was a nothing. And he had made her a nothing. She who had once been a nurse in a hospital had fallen to this. She tried to excuse herself. She had been very tired after a heavy day's duty when he picked her up on the Barberton street, and he had been drunk, but not so drunk as not to know she was alone. The next morning he had produced the sewing machine. She had never seen such a beauty.

Simon did not notice her withdrawal. He pressed his accelerator, feeling he needed a drink quickly. He stopped opposite the hotel.

"Here's a pound. Buy something you want and be back in the car in half an hour." Mrs. Simon took the pound.

More than an hour later he emerged from the hotel, swaggering slightly but otherwise as sober as usual, to find Mrs. Simon sitting alone in the back of the car. He said nothing, thinking she was sulking at him for keeping her waiting.

"Hospital, James," he ordered himself jovially, clambering into the empty front seat.

His bravado left him as soon as he stood again in the cool-smelling entrance.

The matron asked coldly, "Do you want to see the doctor?"

"Yes, ma'am," he muttered. "I'd better."

"All right. He is free now. I'll take you to him."

He dreaded facing the doctor, in case it was the same who had failed to save Lomusa. He feared that then his self-control would break completely.

"Who is the doctor?" he managed to ask.

"Doctor McFadyan."

He gave a long, silent whistle of relief. The doctor, in white coat, received him with bluff cheer and waved him to a chair.

"Hello, Doc."

"Hello, Simon."

They were old acquaintances—not friends. The doctor knew a lot about Simon, more than Simon thought. Still, he was not too bad; in fact, the "Doc" quite liked the "drunken old so-and-so." Forty years' practice in the country had taught him that loneliness and isolation made men a bit queer, and he was too busy to bother much about little peculiarities. He had heard about the wife and wondered what Simon had picked up after she had gone.

"You brought me a real bad case." His Scots accent had not changed in Africa.

"Will she live, Doc?"

"I'm afraid she hasn't a chance." He spoke Sicenga's doom as a commonplace. He had seen too much human suffering to be sentimental, and too much human decency to be callous. You had to accept the inevitability of death.

But Simon, who all along had dreaded being the carrier of such news, almost collapsed. The nightmare of Lomusa's death flooded over him. His eyes filled and his voice was only a whisper as he asked, "What is the matter with her?"

"Encephalitis on top of blackwater. It's usually fatal, unless diagnosed and treated immediately." The doctor grew angry and intense. "They always do this to me. They send the cases that are too far gone for us to cure and then give us the reputation of being a darn sight worse than their own *nyangas*. I might even have had a chance to pull the girl through if I'd got her before she was stuffed with their muck. Now she's so weak she had no strength left to fight. When the hell will they stop practising this witchcraft stuff and believe in Western science?"

Simon no longer believed in "Western science" either, but he was too distracted to argue. He asked a little more about the sickness—what was the name that Doc had said? Spell it, please. Encephalitis. He wrote it down, though he didn't think it would help to tell it to the chief. The doctor described its course in the simplest terms; the cause, he admitted, was uncertain.

Simon left as soon as he could, asking that any urgent message be telephoned through to Tootles' office to be sent to the chief.

Outside, he said to Mrs. Simon, "Come in front."

"No."

"What the hell's eating you? A —— lot of comfort you are."

He accelerated. What did it matter? In Mbabane he stopped to buy food, but neither of them was hungry. As soon as they returned to the shop he went into his office and drank himself into a torpor.

At sunset of that same day, after the cattle had returned from the pasture, a message from Tootles' office arrived at the chief's village and the peace of evening was shattered by the cry for the dead and the scream of a heart-broken woman.

"My child. My child."

Mhau sent the sad news to the husband, whose duty it was to transport the body to his home and arrange the funeral.

Deep was the mourning for Sicenga. But mourning was not enough; the reason for the tragedy had to be discovered, and Bomu's loss had to be made good by her family.

"So you have returned."

"Yes, *Nkosi*."

"What did you hear? Speak, Mpisi."

The hut was dark and quiet, and Mpisi spoke low.

"We have been far, my lord. We began with Baloti, the diviner at the Ingwempisi. We didn't see his truth. He talked like a god and pointed to no one; his words were like froth in a waterfall, without substance. 'The trouble springs from jealousy,' he raved. What trouble does not spring from jealousy? We left him and journeyed through forest and mountains till we came to Incabanga of Namahasha. He is a marvel, a wonder, a wizard! His eyes show that he is inspired. They shine right through you, and nothing is hidden from them. His father and his grandfather were the same, and now as spirits they guide him in wisdom."

"I've heard much about him. Whom did he strike?"

The darkness closed in on Mhau and his trusted men.

Mpisi's voice was without irony. "Those whom we all suspected." A deep pause.

"The mother and her child?"

"The same."

"How did he point them out?"

"He said, 'A mother, but not the mother. A wife of her father.' We agreed. We urged him on and he pushed forward. 'A great wife, daughter of a great man.' He saw her jealousy because her own daughter was not sent as wife to a young chief. The heart boiled. Jealousy showed the witchcraft to her. 'Her child,' he said, 'is also too proud.' "

Family elders had to be informed, and Mpisi was sent to fetch them. Mhau told them, and they, too, were not surprised. It was indeed as they had all known, even before the verdict. Only now it was confirmed by the great doctors with knowledge of secret powers gleaned from strange sources.

The ancient Beta mumbled from toothless jaws, "Drive them away, the witch and her family. How can peace be in a home with such as they flying about at night?"

Lubelo interrupted cringingly, "Pardon me for cutting your tongue, Father, but if you do that at the present time, you will land in the white man's jail."

Another suggested, "Don't tell why banished. Just banish."

Mhau asked, "And do you think that her people will agree? Does not every family deny its own witchcraft? And we have no evidence that the whites will accept. They don't even agree that there are people who can turn into animals and steal the soul from someone asleep. They only believe what their eyes can read in books. They are blind to things of the night."

Beta suggested a compromise. "Build her a village far away from the rest. You can always say you will visit her, though I don't know that that will really help. A witch is not stopped by such a simple trick. She can still throw death from a distance or steal the breath through the wind. A hyena isn't caught in a bird's snare, yet if she didn't live so close to the others jealousy might not wake against them. What do you say, my son?"

Mhau spoke gravely. "It is hard to dismiss a wife and a child who is your own, but I cannot let this evil stay in my village. I think it started many years back when I first saw a baboon on the pinnacle of my daughters' hut. You were with me, Mpisi. Do you remember?"

"Yes, *Nkosi*. I remember it well. It was just before Mputuya struck the prophet and your daughters began to go to school. We hoped you had chased off the witchcraft with your torch, but it seems its light was not strong enough."

Lubelo had another idea: "Why not throw back the witch-craft on the murderers themselves? I know a doctor who works on the grave and fills it with power to seek out the murderer before the sun has set."

"No. I do not like it. It is too powerful and too dangerous, nor will it help that another woman die."

"But it might stop the death of others," continued Lubelo obstinately.

"What person might not kill?" Mhau said with bitterness, as though to himself.

He walked out of the hut for a few minutes and Beta took up his words. "What person might not kill when jealousy awakes?" He and Lubelo looked at each other, and between them ran the strong ripple of mutual dislike and suspicion.

The issue was left undecided, and the elders agreed to meet the next day. One other matter, equally important, but also to be dealt with. Should they send back the cattle to Bomu, or find another girl to take the place of the dead? And if so, whom?

They were unanimous in their agreement that the young chief had behaved well in all respects, except for the suggestion that his wife be taken to the hospital, and even Hlubi had admitted that the witchcraft had eaten her life before she left. Under the circumstances, to return the cattle given by Bomu would be a gross insult; besides, since the sacrificial animals had been offered and accepted, to negate the contract they signified might well evoke further ancestral anger. Now they understood the meaning of the silent death of the first ox; it was a signal to them from the ancestors that evil was afoot and that they should not continue with the ceremony. But as it was, they had complicated it with the blood of the second beast. Obviously, therefore, a girl from Mhau's home had to be supplied to the family of Bomu. Sicenga's little sister, Velapi, on whose arm the symbol of the little co-wife had been tied, was still too young to fill the gap; besides, as Lubelo pointed out, modern girls, irrespective of their birth, were quite prepared to repudiate their parents' promises, and who could tell whether this girl, when she grew up, would not seek assistance from white men to bring her own flesh and blood into trouble?

As at the first selection of a wife from among the daughters of the chief, prospective candidates were canvassed, but this time there was a difference. Lamtana was not even considered. No one spoke her name, and all allusions to her were indirect. The elders sought a girl to link their family in friendly kinship with the bereaved Bomu; and they did not want any further trouble.

They were afraid to mention the possibility that the evil inflicted on Sicenga might be repeated on her successor.

There were a few additional daughters of Mhau from whom to choose, Not-yets who were now Old-enoughs, and, of course, there was Totwa.

Beta supported her claim very strongly by stressing the fine qualities of her mother—her generosity, her ability to live in harmony with those around, her willingness to accept subordination in the harem. He concluded, "The girl Totwa has always followed the path of her mother, and from her she could have acquired no evil."

The crafty Lubelo agreed that all this was true, but argued

that it was therefore a pity to remove such a source of joy from a home stricken with grief.

Mhau cut the discussion short with brutal abruptness. "Totwa is my choice, and she will have to go soon or we might have another case of a princess with child. A girl can't wait to marry till she is too old for children. I think as you do,"—he turned to Beta—"and will speak to her mother."

Nabo Totwa knew indirectly about her daughter's relationship with the leader of the regiment and would willingly have allowed her to marry him if she chose to do so. This mother had no ambition to see her daughter wedded against her inclination, no matter how important the man might be.

She called the girl and, without any beating about the bush, informed her of the council's decision. To her astonishment, Totwa, who had a shrewd notion of all that had been going on, was quite excited at the prospect. It was clear that she was fond of her lover, but she always regarded him as a lover, and, though she had not yet realized it, she had begun to tire of him. She was lovely, mischievous and flighty as well as sweet and warm-hearted, and the thought of going to Bomu excited and attracted her. Possibly, had the elders not made their suggestion, she would have married her lover, with her parents' consent, when he sent along the necessary cattle; she would not have liked to hurt him by taking the initiative in rejection. Now the decision was made for her; it was an act not of cruelty but of duty, and she trusted that he, too, would see it in that light. Nabo Totwa was therefore able to tell Mhau that Totwa was perfectly agreeable.

That night Mhau sent for Sicenga's mother. It was the first time that he had been alone with her since her daughter's death, and as she sat opposite him he turned his head away and his stomach contracted with pity at the dark signs of mourning. She had torn down her lovely high bun for sorrow and bound her hair up roughly so that a huge hole gaped at the top. Around her waist were heavy ropes of mourning. Her body, usually glowing with fat and health, was dull and unwashed.

"You are not well, my wife?" he asked kindly.

"It is not the flesh that is ill, my lord. To lose a baby is heavy, but to lose a child already grown kills the heart. That girl of mine I loved greatly."

"We all did."

"No, not all. Our love woke others' hate. What did Mpisi say?"

"He said exactly that."

She didn't speak, but began weeping quietly, wiping away her tears from her nose with big heavy movements of the backs of her hands.

He told her of the council's selection of Totwa, and she expressed approval. "She and my child always felt for one another," she said, and she went on to ask without much interest what he would do about the trouble-makers.

"I will drive them away to the mother's people."

Nabo Sicenga commented, "It will not help me now. My child will not return. I feel killed by loneliness."

"There are still others. And I am here." He would have liked to comfort her as best he knew, but, since she was still in mourning, to sleep with her would harm them both.

She seemed to read his thoughts, and smiled for the first time. "I will go now. Do not waste yourself, my lord."

"No," and he laughed richly. "I will leave you."

"Go well, my husband."

Though no one accused Nabo Lamtana or Lamtana directly, it soon became clear that they, particularly the mother, were considered guilty. Soon Nabo Lamtana almost took it for granted that she was, in fact, guilty. It gave her a feeling of great power. Perhaps she really was a flying witch. She had never really liked Sicenga, and though she could not recall exactly how she might have killed her, she knew that one could not always remember what one's spirit did in the night. She would enjoy being sent home where she could lord it over her brother's wives, but she did not want her family to have to protest against the slanderous accusation of witchcraft. News had reached her that her old father was not well, and she herself sent to Mhau and asked that she be permitted to go to him on a visit. Her husband tried to conceal his relief and gladly granted permission, suggesting that Lamtana should accompany her. When Lamtana heard of this, she felt a deep hatred and resentment and swore to herself that she would not go to her mother's people, to be the butt of their unspoken criticism; but neither could she remain alone in her father's home as the witch who had killed his eldest daughter.

In view of the general hostility towards her and her mother, the announcement that Totwa had been chosen to replace Sicenga had come as no surprise. Nabo Lamtana merely commented, with a shaft of her former quick malice, "The husband got more than he bargained for, and, anyway, he had sent too many cattle in the first place."

Lamtana, who knew how deeply she would miss Totwa, decided after long and bitter consideration that the only escape from disgrace and loneliness was to go to Feka's home; there, at least, she thought, she would be welcomed and respected, and she would have her child.

So one morning, without saying a word to anyone about her decision, she went there, and from the gate she saw Nabo Feka in her yard. And she was sure that Nabo Feka spied her coming. But when she arrived, no one was there to greet her. Lamtana waited. She waited quite a long time. Perhaps she was wrong, and had not seen. She called. With deliberate slowness Nabo Feka came out of her hut and stretched her loose-skinned yet muscular arms, as though she were alone. Finally she looked at Lamtana and curtly acknowledged her presence.

Lamtana could not believe that this was indeed her welcome till the older woman enquired from her as from a stranger about her family. A weakening emptiness made it hard for Lamtana to reply.

"I am well."

The response was silence.

All she realized was that *she* was now the unwanted. She brought herself to enquire about Sipiwo.

"He is herding the calves."

Was he well?

"Yes." The older woman was watching her now with undisguised suspicion and hostility. The face of Timba's mother, ugly with dislike, appeared for a minute in the doorway, then withdrew into the hut. There was nothing more to say.

"Stay well."

"Go well."

From Nabo Feka's, she went straight to Simon's, where she arrived physically and mentally exhausted. Mrs. Simon made her strong tea, sweet and thick with condensed milk, and insisted on her sitting and drinking it before she would let her speak.

Things were not going well with Mrs. Simon, either. Since the day in Mbabane when she had sat in the back of the car, there had been an increasing estrangement between her and her husband. He was drinking more than ever, and spent less and less time in their bungalow. One day he had driven alone to Mbabane and returned the following day, and she did not ask and he did not say what he had done or where he had slept. Even when they were together he seemed to ignore her presence, though he never maltreated her or even swore at her.

When Lamtana came, Mrs. Simon was in a mood of bleak rebellion, and while Lamtana slowly drank her hot tea she poured out her grievances.

"I'm tired of sitting here like a prisoner. If I had the chance I'd leave him and let him look after himself, or find another 'housekeeper.'" Lamtana felt quite sorry for Simon, but more sorry for her friend.

After a time Mrs. Simon said, "I've been talking about my troubles; what has been happening to you?"

As Lamtana recounted her tale, ending with her visit to Feka's home, her despair gave way to anger. What right had his mother to treat her like that? She would never, never again be prepared to live with her and look after her. It served her right.

But where would she live? Suddenly came the inspiration, blinding and dazzling. "I will go away. I will go to Goli. I will find Feka, and if he doesn't want me, I won't care. I will work for myself in the town. I am afraid for my own life in this place where everyone hates me."

"Your father will bring you back."

"No, he won't. I'll be in a white man's place. Even if he finds me, he can't force me back. I will be free." Passionately she declared, "I must leave my home. It wants me no longer. There is nothing there for me but hatred. She who loved me and whom I loved best is dead. Totwa is going to be married. My mother goes her own way. I am not a slave to be taken by this one and that one, or a stone that does not suffer. I am a person. I am Nkosi Lamtana Dlamini. I will go away. I will go to Goli." Impulsively she put out her hands to Mrs. Simon. "Come with me, my sister."

Mrs. Simon drew in her breath sharply, stunned by the enormity of an idea which, though previously expressed by herself, she had never really considered a possibility or reduced to the specific.

"What would we do in Goli? On what would we live? How could we even get there?"

Lamtana replied obstinately, "I will get there. I have some shillings and I have my strength. Will you come? Think of all we can do in Goli."

Mrs. Simon looked round, her plain little face puckered by conflicting thoughts. What would she do without all her possessions? The double bed. The floral basin. The rug. The sewing machine. Could she leave all these behind?

Lamtana was waiting for the answer, her entire being suddenly revitalized and beautiful with hope of freedom, entranced by the pictures of her own imagination.

Mrs. Simon looked again at her sewing machine. It was a fine, reliable machine, but it gave her only what she put into it. Nothing more. It was a good tool. There were other machines. She found herself saying, "I could sew for white people and earn us money."

"Of course you could. And I—I could work and learn white people's ways."

But then Mrs. Simon again grew cautious. "No. I can't go. It is too dangerous. We might be killed on the way."

"I am already dead. How can I live when I am not wanted?"

"But we won't know where to go. We will have no friends."

"We will be together. We will help each other."

"We don't even know the road."

"Couldn't we go through Barberton? Think how pleased all the nurses would be to see you again."

This tempted her. She shut her eyes and clucked. "It would be wonderful to see my old friends again." Then, remembering the circumstances of her abrupt departure, she became less sure. "But perhaps they won't be so pleased."

"Of course they will. You never did *them* any harm."

"Perhaps they're all dead or gone away."

"Somebody's always left. Don't be afraid, please, my friend."

The entry of Simon interrupted their plotting, but only for a short while. He merely wagged a heavy finger at Lamtana and went straight past his wife to the bedroom. Mrs. Simon turned away. Soon loud and regular snores reported his condition to the woman.

As Mrs. Simon listened her eyes narrowed, her body stiffened, and she raised her head high. She said, "He's not a person any more. I want nothing from him. He treats me like a servant who cooks his food, and if I go he won't starve." Her contempt for him had given her a dignity and self-respect she had never before possessed. "Yes, Lamtana, it is time I left him."

Controlling her joy, Lamtana asked simply, "Will you tell him?"

"Never. He would never agree." Without bitterness, but perhaps a little too harshly, she summed him up. "He likes best the things he can never have and the things that he has lost. He would want me to stay most if he heard I was going."

"All right. We must go without saying good-bye."

Lamtana would have liked to leave the following day, but that was a Wednesday and the bus to Barberton did not go till Friday. Mrs. Simon was glad of that; though she felt contempt for Simon, she had a deep sense of duty and wanted to put his house in good order before abandoning him. Also, she had received part payment for the trousseau of a Christian girl, and felt obliged to complete the wedding dress in fulfilment since she was taking the money with her. Nor did she want to be hurried—hers was a decision of boredom, not of active pain.

They laid their plans with the greatest care. It was easy enough for Lamtana to leave her home and go to the shop, but Mrs. Simon would have to wait till her man was out or otherwise engaged before she could move. They arranged that Lamtana was to come early on Friday morning and find out the position. If Simon was in the shop, she was to keep him occupied in showing her goods from the far corner till Mrs. Simon was out of sight and on the road to the bus stop. Lamtana would then join her, and they would catch the bus together. If he was out, Mrs. Simon would know his destination and avoid the road along which he would travel. It was unlikely that anyone meeting the two women would suspect that Mrs. Simon had run away, knowing how carefully in the past Simon had watched over her, and how she had cared for him.

They discussed exactly what they would take with them. Lamtana's priceless possessions were few and could be tied easily in a bundle. Mrs. Simon had to choose what to take from her rich variety of goods. She was most reluctant to leave the machine. After all, it was hers. He had given it to her, and she had given him service all the years. But finally she agreed that it was too heavy to carry in addition to all the other things she loved, which would fill an entire suitcase. She had the bright idea that if anyone asked what was in the suitcase, she would reply it was the trousseau of the Christian girl—for whom everyone knew she had been sewing—who lived at a mission station on the road to the Peak, on the way to Barberton. At Barberton Mrs. Simon would seek out her friends. Over the years with Simon, she had saved fifteen pounds, three shillings, and sixpence, which she kept in a little black box in the bottom drawer of the cupboard. With all that money, and Lamtana's shillings, they could travel by bus and train and have enough over until they got work in Goli.

Everything was settled at last.

"Why didn't we think of it before?" Lamtana ended happily.

She returned home, successfully hiding her excitement. She longed to tell Totwa, but it was too great a risk. Besides, if the family discovered that Totwa had known, she would be held guilty and punished.

The days till Friday were almost unendurable. She had an intense longing to see her son before she went away. Would she ever see him again? The doubt was a spear in her heart. Not that he would cling to her, she reminded herself bitterly; she had lost her claim to his affection. But she wanted to hold him to her. If only she could explain that she did love him. But she must not go to him. She would not go to him. Instead, she left early in the morning to weed her mother's field, and returned at night physically weary. On the way she passed a neglected garden of Nabo Sicenga's and would gladly have spent her strength cleaning it for her, but knew that she did not even dare set foot in it. And she could not bridge the gulf between herself and her own mother—was her mother really a witch, or, like herself, a victim of malice and suspicion? And if her mother had witchcraft in her—not the deliberate kind, but the kind that ran in the blood—was she, Lamtana, not also tainted?

Sleep came in troubled bouts. The second night, after Totwa, lying beside her, grumbled, "Why are you throwing yourself about?" she was afraid to stir and lay waiting for dawn while her mind revolved desperately in a maze from which there was no exit. "What is it that stops me from sleeping? What pushes me awake at night? Is there really witchcraft in me? I don't want to harm anyone. Why am I hated?"

She was afraid that Mrs. Simon might change her mind. If that happened, Lamtana began to wonder if she would have the courage to go alone. At times she dreaded the sheer physical vulnerability of being a woman. From deep in her memory of childhood came the nightmare recollection of the mad-eyed prophet feeling the women in the dark hut.

On Thursday night Lamtana announced that she was going to Simon's the next day, to buy salt and candles with ground-nuts from her garden. Before she left, her mother gave her an extra two shillings and sixpence for a few things she herself required. Ostentatiously, Lamtana produced the cloth in which she would wrap the nuts, and soon left with a neat bundle balanced on her head. The nuts had been miraculously transformed into her last school uniform, a red comb, a mirror presented by Feka when they were still at school together, the bright multi-coloured glass bangles which her mother had given her years and years ago, a few other odds and ends, and her "Books of Thots."

She went straight to the shop and noticed at once that Simon was not there and that the office door was open. Having greeted the assistant and purchased a large cake of soap, she asked in a voice that she tried to make casual, "Has Simon gone out already?"

"Out! He hasn't come in yet. He left yesterday evening and I think he has forgotten the way home!" The assistant laughed cheerfully at this idea.

"Do you want him?"

"No. I just asked."

"Do you want to buy something else, *Nkosatana?* This clothing would love you," and he began to bring down his whole stock of new material.

She tried not to show her impatience, to carry on the usual banter that made shopping a delightfully sociable niche in which the exchange of goods and cash could be made to appear a minor—but essential—detail. Finally she excused herself, saying, "I will see Mrs. Simon now."

The assistant watched her with a slight stirring of curiosity. She often came to the shop first and went from there to the house, but to-day, somehow, she seemed different. His attention was distracted by a customer.

Mrs. Simon had seen Lamtana enter the shop and came tripping to meet her at the door of her house. She was wearing a brown winter coat and a pink straw hat for travelling.

Lamtana could not confess her relief, but exclaimed, *"Hau!* Gladys, you look beautiful."

Gladys giggled nervously. "We must be quick. Come on and help me shut my case. It's too full. I can't shut it myself. We must hurry."

She had packed to the brim, with the pillow slip embroidered "Jesus Loves Me" on the top. Lamtana sat on the lid and pressed down firmly, and the lock closed with a snap.

Speaking more quickly than usual, Mrs. Simon reported that Simon had again gone to Mbabane and stayed away for the night and she did not know when he would be back. Last time he had returned at eleven A.M. and slept till six P.M. He had then demanded his breakfast! If he stayed away as long this time, they were safe. But if not . . . If he found them at the bus stop, Mrs. Simon said finally, she did not know what she would do. She told Lamtana that she had packed when he left, then unpacked, then finally she repacked at dawn, and she put on her travelling clothes when she saw Lamtana arrive. Lamtana, realizing they had to get away before Gladys again changed her mind, almost pushed her out of the door.

Quite a few people saw them leave, but no one dreamed that they were embarking on a great adventure. Lamtana offered to carry the suitcase. At first Mrs. Simon refused, and struggled a short way with it in her hand like a white woman. But it was too heavy, and, without even asking this time, Lamtana lifted it from her, gave Mrs. Simon the bundle, and put the suitcase on her own head. Carrying it easily and gracefully, she walked ahead to the bus stop. Her heart was thudding with excitement, and whereas Mrs. Simon looked—as she felt—both guilty and nervous, Lamtana was now altogether eager.

At the bus stop she put down the suitcase and looked back along the path to her home, and she suddenly recollected the day that she had stood on the ant heap to watch a tall man and a tall boy leaving for the distant city, and she relived the pain that she had felt when Feka first went away, and she experienced a sudden urge to see him again.

The sound of a car in the distance drew a frightened gasp from Mrs. Simon, who scurried behind the shelter with Lamtana following her carrying the suitcase and the bundle. But it was not Simon, and when the danger was over and they emerged, Mrs. Simon said fervently, "God is helping us." In a few minutes more they would be safe. Lamtana dared not trust herself to speak, but laughed loudly.

When at last the bus arrived, she helped Mrs. Simon up the high single step into the section at the back reserved for non-whites, climbed in lightly after her, and took a seat beside her. The driver closed the door. Clutching her bundle and smiling with excitement, Lamtana looked out of the narrow window at the beautiful country. The bus lurched forward, nearly throwing her off the narrow wooden seat. A few bright-faced, raggedy children ran to the roadside to wave to the bus as it passed. Lamtana waved back at them and whispered, "Stay well, my children."

Simon passed their bus on the road, arriving home about half an hour after it had left. He walked in without noticing Mrs. Simon's absence and threw himself on the bed.

When he woke several hours later, he called, "Gladys. Bring me some coffee."

He waited for a few minutes and, on hearing no sound, repeated his order. Silence again.

Only then did it strike him that the room looked different. Where were the china shepherdess, the embroidered pillow, the photograph of Gladys in nurse's uniform?

He staggered from the bed and yelled, "Gladys. What the hell are you doing?"

He stumbled to the shop and asked the assistant, point-blank, "Where is Mrs. Simon?"

The assistant told him all he knew. Simon listened without a single interruption until the end, and then said in a dazed voice, "Lamtana asked for me and then went with her."

The assistant didn't correct him, but watched with pity and understanding as he went into the office and closed the door behind him.

The news had already reached the chief's homestead, where the perfidious Lubelo had been the first to hear it and had rushed with it to Mhau, together with a suggestion that the police be immediately informed so that they could stop the women at the Transvaal border and send them back. But Mhau refused to be pushed into a hasty decision. He sent for Beta and Nabo Sicenga, and closeted together in his private hut, they discussed the matter fully. All agreed that no action be taken by the family.

No one knows who told Nabo Lamtana, but that same evening she sent a message to the chief asking for an escort to accompany her the following day to her father's home. Mhau agreed willingly and delegated the unpopular task to the ever-servile Mpisi.